MW01027755

SABIKUI BISCO

MIRACULOUS FINAL CUT

6

SHINJI COBKUBO

Illustration by
K AKAGISHI

World Concept Art by
mocha

SABIKO

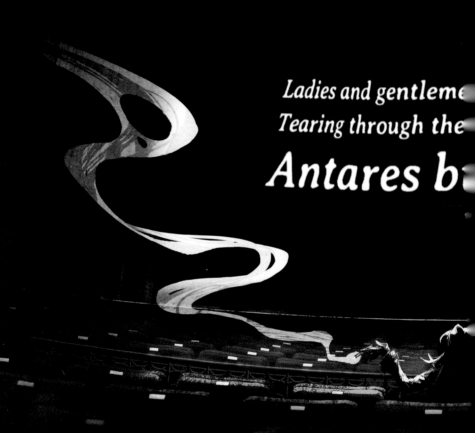

Ladies and gentleme
Tearing through the

Antares b

    THE RUST WIND EATS AWAY AT THE WORLD ——————

BISCO

...old.
...ss night,
...s crimson!

—Director **Kenji Kurokawa**

A BOY WITH A BOW MATCHES ITS FEROCITY

SABIKUI BISCO

SHINJI COBKUBO

Illustration by
K AKAGISHI

World Concept Art by
mocha

The Rust Wind eats away at the world. A boy with a bow matches its ferocity.

SABIKUI BISCO

6

Miraculous Final Cut

SHINJI COBKUBO

Illustration by
K Akagishi

World Concept Art by
mocha (@mocha708)

YEN
ON

NEW YORK

SABIKUI BISCO 6

Shinji Cobkubo

Translation by Jake Humphrey

This book is a work of fiction. Names, characters, places, and incidents are the product of the author's imagination or are used fictitiously. Any resemblance to actual events, locales, or persons, living or dead, is coincidental.

SABIKUI BISCO Vol. 6
©Shinji Cobkubo 2020
Edited by Dengeki Bunko
First published in Japan in 2020 by KADOKAWA CORPORATION, Tokyo.
English translation rights arranged with KADOKAWA CORPORATION, Tokyo, through
TUTTLE-MORI AGENCY, INC., Tokyo.

English translation © 2023 by Yen Press, LLC

Yen On
150 West 30th Street, 19th Floor
New York, NY 10001

Visit us at yenpress.com † facebook.com/yenpress † twitter.com/yenpress
yenpress.tumblr.com † instagram.com/yenpress

First Yen On Edition: November 2023
Edited by Yen On Editorial: Emma McClain, Payton Campbell
Designed by Yen Press Design: Wendy Chan

Yen On is an imprint of Yen Press, LLC.
The Yen On name and logo are trademarks of Yen Press, LLC.

The publisher is not responsible for websites (or their content) that are not owned by the publisher.

Library of Congress Cataloging-in-Publication Data
Names: Cobkubo, Shinji, author. | Akagishi K. illustrator. | mocha, illustrator. |
    Humphrey, Jake, translator.
Title: Sabikui bisco / Shinji Cobkubo ; illustration by K Akagishi ; world concept art by mocha ;
    translation by Jake Humphrey.
Other titles: Sabikui bisco. English
Description: First Yen On edition. | New York, NY : Yen On, 2021- |
Identifiers: LCCN 2021046139 | ISBN 9781975336813 (v. 1 ; trade paperback) |
    ISBN 9781975336837 (v. 2 ; trade paperback) | ISBN 9781975336851 (v. 3 ; trade paperback) |
    ISBN 9781975336875 (v. 4 ; trade paperback) | ISBN 9781975336899 (v. 5 ; trade paperback) |
    ISBN 9781975336912 (v. 6 ; trade paperback)
Subjects: LCGFT: Science fiction.
Classification: LCC PL868.5.O65 S3413 2021 | DDC 895.63/6—dc23/eng/20211001
LC record available at https://lccn.loc.gov/2021046139

ISBNs: 978-1-9753-3691-2 (paperback)
        978-1-9753-3692-9 (ebook)

10 9 8 7 6 5 4 3 2 1

LSC-C

Printed in the United States of America

The Japanese edition of this novel
includes bonus manga.
Flip to the beginning of the manga,
read right to left, and enjoy!

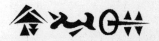

Dust-covered scraps tumbled across the ground in the cold autumn wind.

END THE FEAR!
 SAY NO TO TYRANNY!

Each was filled with bullet holes, scorched, and splattered with blood. They danced in the wind like the flags of the Kurokawa administration up above, before floating out of sight.

Once, Karakusa Street was a bustling avenue, filled with vendors and restaurants, purveyors of vice and corrupted missionaries, and salvagers returning with their hauls. It was a place where the voices of buyers and hawkers drowned out all else.

But now the streets lay silent. To borrow the words of a passing peddler:

"This place is a ghost town…"

Indeed, the city of Imihama was haunted by specters. They wore rabbit-headed masks with fixed smiles. With machine guns at the ready, they patrolled the streets.

The Immies were a symbol of oppression in this city, and they were untouchable. One of them prodded a cowering civilian with his gun and shouted, "Keep movin', punk!"

"Citizens! It's screening time! Get out here!"

A black Immie, this district's leader, barked an order and fired his machine gun into the air. The people hiding in their homes came out onto the street instantly and lined up, trembling with fright.

"One minute, thirteen seconds," the black Immie snarled. "Too slow! And what's with those sniveling faces? You're about to see a movie! Let's see some big happy grins, or else!"

The people all forced nervous-looking grins. The punishment for unhappiness, they knew, was death. The black Immie looked at their twitching faces, satisfied.

"Very good," he said, lowering his gun. "Always keep a smile on your face, just like us."

"That's a mask!" one of them shouted.

"You're all Kurokawa's goddamn lapdogs," muttered another.

"Hey, no talking!" the black Immie barked. "Line up!"

"Please! My son has been working on one essay after another for forty-eight hours straight! If he doesn't get some rest, he'll collapse!"

"He should be proud to die in pursuit of his work. For an artist, there is no greater honor. Now start walking, or I'll start shooting."

With no means to defy the Immies, the townspeople grudgingly hobbled over to the location of the screening. The cameras lining the streets watched them cautiously with metallic eyes, leaving no hope of escape.

"Urgh. I can't take any more!"

"Sit still! You'll watch until the end!"

"Someone, please, help me!"

"Tighten the straps! Give him the extended course. Leave him foaming at the mouth."

At the Imihama central cinema, the projectors never stopped. The civilians were strapped to their seats, their eyes held open by torturous devices attached to their faces. They knew there was no point in resisting, and so resigned themselves to sit and watch, sobbing and groaning all the while.

…However, at the back, behind them all, sat one figure whose tears were very much inspired by the view on the big screen.

* * *

"...Hic... Sob..."

"...*I just...never knew how to say good-bye.*"

"...Has there ever been a line so beautiful? It's like it's speaking directly to me..."

"...Governor Kurokawa. The program is about to end."

"Shut up, you idiot! Can't you see I'm invested?!"

Kurokawa slapped the unfortunate black Immie, then with no trace of her earlier tears, stretched out her back and groaned.

"Oh dear. Now you've ruined the mood. But I suppose it's been a long day. How have the citizens fared?"

"A few more deaths and blackouts than usual, but nothing to be concerned about. They're all watching intently."

"Excellent. Soon the entire country will be under my control."

Kurokawa ran a hand through her long, spiky hair, rough like a pine tree, and stood from her luxury seat. Her black lamé dress exposed her back and cleavage and was slitted to offer a scintillating peek at her long, fair legs. Her shawl was crafted from genuine Shimobukian snow leopard fur, and her extravagant hat just screamed money, power, and pride. The entire getup made her seem even less approachable than usual.

"We'll continue this program until all the dusty ideas of old Japan have been wiped clean from their brains," Kurokawa declared. "Be careful. And don't screw up."

"Yes, ma'am."

"Refill."

"Yes, ma'am."

The Immie produced a bottle of grape Fanta and topped up the wineglass in Kurokawa's impatient hand. The blackhearted governor downed it in a single gulp before tossing the glass to the ground, shattering it. Then she turned and headed for the door, humming a tune as she went.

"*Hmm-hm-hm-hmmm, ♪ hmm-hm-hmm.*"

"..."

"*Hmm-hm-hm-hmmm.* ♪ ...You. What theme?"

"*Indiana Jones.*"

"Well done. Have a raise, and keep up the good work."

"Thank you."

Kurokawa then left the screening hall and vaulted into the back seat of a waiting AC Cobra, stretching her legs and crossing them seductively.

"Everything is ready," she said. "All we need now is the main actor."

She snapped her fingers, and the driver hit the gas, ferrying the governor down flag-lined streets toward the prefectural bureau.

* * *

One year ago, on this very day, Pawoo, the Whirling Steel, was bested, and Imihama was subjected to a horrifying broadcast depicting their raven-haired leader licking the crimson-heeled boot of a mysterious woman.

"Hello, my dutiful citizens. I do hope you've kept yourselves busy in my absence."

Her body and voice were female, but no citizen could forget the pitch-black eyes that lurked behind those signature sunglasses.

"Sorry I didn't call. I kinda had my hands full, y'know, coming back from the dead. But not to worry. As of today, Nekoyanagi's iron rule is over. She will return to the Vigilante Corps...and I, Kenji Kurokawa, will be taking her place."

The evil governor, Kurokawa, had returned.

On that day, the streets were flooded with Immies, men in black suits and masks of Kurokawa's own design. They made sure the people submitted to a new and unfathomable plan of the governor's invention.

Named the "Thought Cleansing Program," the policy saw that citizens were provided with videos and printed material curated by the Kurokawa administration. They were required to regularly consume these materials and submit a twenty-thousand-word essay, and if they failed to score sufficient grades, they would be punished.

For modern people who lived hand to mouth, this requirement was practically physical torture, but any attempts at rebellion were quickly put down by the Vigilante Corps, led by Pawoo. Her personality had shifted completely from the benevolent governor the citizens knew, and her merciless and violent crackdowns crushed their spirits.

It was a true dictatorship—a wicked regime.

Meanwhile, on the national stage, the new Kurokawa had an even sharper mind than the last. She partnered up with Matoba Heavy Industries, the powerhouse dominating Japanese weapons development, and with a steady supply of animal weapons, she unleashed a blitzkrieg the likes of which the nation had never seen. One by one, prefectures fell to her military tactics. First the region around Kyoto to the west, then the northern reaches, and finally the beaches of the northwestern coast. In the blink of an eye, Kurokawa solidified her grasp on Japan's central territories, and her sphere of influence was still growing. Nationwide, fearful citizens scribbled their essays, living in fear of the governor's enforcers and their perpetual, rabbit-headed grins.

* * *

A few citizens gathered at a fountain outside the screening hall.

"Finally, it's over. My eyeballs feel like they're gonna crumble to dust."

"Don't forget, we still have the essay to write when we get home…"

"If I have to look at one more sheet of lined paper, I think I'm gonna hurl."

A full two hours after Kurokawa exited the building, the citizens were finally allowed to leave. After this, their essays would be carefully checked for signs that their ideological cleansing was proceeding as planned.

The citizens were in a state of total exhaustion. All this was obvious to the pink-haired jellyfish girl sitting in the center of the plaza.

"...Aaahhh, finally over, huh?"

The petite girl, dressed in a black suit, perched on the rim of the dried-up fountain and stretched her arms and legs with a yawn.

"I'm gonna die of boredom," she moaned. "But at least I don't gotta watch the screenings."

"Miss Ochagama!" said an assistant Immie, running up to her. "We've finished counting the citizens. Two failed to show up to the screening, one ran while being transported, and as for those who fainted or forgot to turn off their mobile phones..."

"Aah, who cares?! I ain't yer mommy! Figure it out yourself!"

The Immie gave a polite bow, displaying an impressive dedication to formality clearly lacking in his superior, and returned to his work. Tirol watched him go with a bored look on her face, before hopping off her butt and onto the cobbles with a flutter of her tentacle-like braids.

She squinted into the wind, surveying the town. She had already grown used to the city's new appearance—its buildings and even the prefectural bureau itself remodeled in a Hollywood style. She no longer batted an eye at the Neo-Kurokawa administration's flags flying from every mast.

Can't believe it's been a year.

As a traveling merchant, Tirol possessed very little in the way of political power. Fortunately, she had so little integrity and self-respect that the governor was eager to overlook her past betrayals, and it wasn't hard to leverage her experience—six months as an Immie, two years as Chief Engineer at Matoba—to wrangle her way into the highly coveted position of Inspector Immie.

Every day's such a bore. I'm gonna sneak out and go clothes shopping.

After a quick glance around to ensure no one saw her, Tirol turned to leave. But just as she did...

"Miss Ochagama!"

Erk!

"A delivery just came in at the west gate. It's a little ahead of schedule, but there's twenty-four carts in all. Shall I call them over?"

"Customs duty, huh? Sure. Just gotta give it the ol' ocular patdown, right?"

The Immie spoke into his transceiver. "The site is secure. Bring them in." Tirol heard a *"Roger"* from the other end. Seconds later, the floor began to rumble as two dozen hippo-drawn wagons filled the square. Tirol poked her head inside one and saw it was stuffed with cameras, tripods, and lighting equipment.

"Yep, first one's okay! Send it through!"

"Miss Ochagama, your stamp of approval, please."

"Here ya go," said Tirol, whipping out her jellyfish-shaped rubber stamp and pressing it to the hippo's neck.

"Thank you," said the assistant Immie. Then, to the driver, "Head to the bureau! And be careful; that's delicate machinery!"

Tirol watched the hippo go, before casting a cursory glance over the contents of the other wagons and marking them all with her seal.

What's with all the filming equipment? Why not guns or drugs? ...Eh, whatever. The sooner this is done, the sooner I can go home.

Soon Tirol reached the last wagon, and parted the curtain to take a look inside. Just as she did, however, her sleepy amber eyes gleamed.

...What's that smell?

She recognized it.

...Mushrooms...?

Only a merchant like Tirol could have detected that faintest of whiffs. It certainly didn't belong to any conceivable kind of recording equipment, nor did it smell like rust. This was something with life, born of the earth. Tirol strained her eyes, staring into the mountain of tripods, when...

...something stared back at her.

"Eep!!"

No, two somethings, jade-green and gleaming. Tirol let out a squeal and went tumbling backward out of the wagon as if someone had pushed her, toppling a pile of wide-angle lenses on her way out.

"Whoooa?!"

""?!""

Two assistant Immies noticed her distress and ran over.

"M-Miss Ochagama?! What happened? Are you okay?!"

"Is something in there?!"

From her stricken expression, they could tell this was no laughing matter.

"Leave it to us!" one of them said. Then to the other, "You, take the right side."

The two of them took a deep breath and peered inside the wagon.

Oh, shit...

"...Huh?! You're...!"

"It's them! Sound the alarm! Sound—"

"Nrraaagh!!"

Tirol leaped into the air, pulling out a crowbar she kept at her hip and bringing it down on the head of the Immie trying to call for help.

"Gyugh!"

Then she spun in midair, delivering a second blow to her other assistant just as he turned in shock.

"Byaagh!"

The two Immies twirled before collapsing to the ground. Tirol picked up the walkie-talkie.

"Erm... Number seven and number eight just passed out from stress! ...Hmm? What's that? Oh, I guess you're right, it does happen all the time! Not really worth raisin' the alarm over, huh? Heh-heh-heh... Sorryyy! Ignore that! Over!"

Tirol ended the call and collapsed onto her back, exhausted. Just then, two boys popped their heads from the back of the wagon, peering down at her curiously.

It was a curse. It had to be. Every time she saw those two baby-faced rascals, it meant Tirol's peaceful days were at an end and a whirlwind of adventure was about to begin.

"What's eatin' her? All I did was look at her," said the first.

"It must be psychosomatic," offered the second. "One look at your face, and she started having a fit."

"Would it kill you to show some respect?!" the first roared back. "What am I, a ghost?!"

The boys' banter was a familiar refrain by now. As it rang in her ears, Tirol rocked herself upright, her mind racing so fast in the face of this danger, it was making her dizzy. She steeled her nerves and faced them. Then...

""Yo.""

"Go 'Yo' yourself, ya bozos!!"

Tirol pounced upon the duo like a cat, slapping their faces back and forth and sending all three tumbling back into the wagon.

"Owwww! That hurt, Tirol!"

"That ain't no way to greet your two oldest friends. Where's your humanity?"

"You two have no right to talk about my humanity after dragging my life through the mud!" Tirol retorted in a hushed yell. The two boys took one look at her frenzied eyes, then turned toward each other.

"Why did ya turn up *here*, of all places?! You know Kurokawa's scouring the country for you! Do you have any idea what she'll do when she finds out you've fallen right into her lap like a couple of brainless morons?!"

As Bisco was about to deliver an angry retort, Milo placed his hand on his partner's shoulder and said calmly, "Listen, Tirol. We can see this place is under some serious martial law. There're cameras in the streets, and the citizens are fighting for their lives. We can't help them alone... That's why we came to you."

"To me? What for?"

"Well..." Milo faltered. "W-we...thought you might be able to help us..."

"Help you?!" Tirol yelled, forgetting the need for secrecy. Thinking quickly, Bisco clapped his hand over her mouth. Tirol's whole face was crimson with anger; she was barely able to keep herself under control.

"*Hee-hoo.* Calm down. *Hee-hoo.* A merchant must maintain a steady temper..."

"That's a weird breathing technique," noted Bisco. "You tryin' to give birth?"

"I-I'm sorry, Tirol, but we didn't have anyone else to—!"

"Sit!"

""Yes, ma'am!!""

Tirol squinted at the submissive boys, a murmur of discontent escaping her lips. Though by all appearances still annoyed, in her mind Tirol was already working on a plan.

"We'll have to hurry," she said. "HQ'll send over an Immie supervisor soon to see what the holdup is. If they find out I'm dawdling on the job, they'll wring my neck!"

"Can't we just beat 'em up?" asked Bisco, offering his unique perspective on the matter.

"Shut up!" yelled Tirol. Then, precisely four seconds later, a light bulb lit up above her head, and she poked her face outside the back of the wagon.

"...It's an old trick," she muttered, "but I guess we ain't got no choice."

She looked down at the ground, taking in the two Immies rendered unconscious by her crowbar. The rabbit masks' big brown eyes cast their vacant gaze up toward the early autumn sky.

1

Tirol swiped her employee ID through the reader, and the screen displayed the words *"Have a nice Friday!"* spoken by a cartoon Kurokawa just three heads high.

"Miss Tirol Ochagama. Everything seems to be in order," said the pretty receptionist at the employee dorm, after she'd read the confirmation on the screen and bowed slightly. "Thank you for your hard work. Your room has been cleaned in your absence."

"Thanks a million. Enjoy yer evening."

"Erm, one minute…"

With a perplexed look, the receptionist shifted her gaze over to the two figures standing behind Tirol. There were two Immies, a red one and a blue one. The blue one was a perfect example of his kind, with a clean and tidy suit and a perfectly tied necktie. The other one, however, well…

The head, for a start, was oddly skewed and distorted. One of the ears had been partially torn, and stuffing was falling out. His suit was wrinkled and creased, but the most bizarre element was his tie: It looked like a barbarian had fastened it, thinking it was meant to protect the neck rather than serve as mere decoration. The whole ensemble looked like an artist's interpretation of a wild and undomesticated Immie.

"What?" barked Tirol. "If it's company shares, I don't buy into that crud."

"N-no," said the receptionist, roused from her staring by Tirol's words. "I was just looking at your companions. You see, I'm afraid regular Immies—those of Class C and below—are forbidden from entering these dorms other than for official business…"

"Well, there's no problem, then. They *are* here on business."

"And what might that business be…?"

"Come on, lady. You really gonna make me say it? I got needs like any woman. After a long, hard day of lickin' the boot, sometimes you just wanna blow off steam with two guys at the same time. You got a problem with that?"

"Er… Um… N-no!" stammered the receptionist, suddenly red in the face. "I'm sorry for interrupting your…er…your meeting. H-have a nice weekend…"

"Oh, and cancel the cleanin' tomorrow. We're gonna be busy till Monday."

With that, Tirol marched over to the elevator, the two boys in tow. Once the doors closed, she let out a deep breath.

"…Phew. That was close." She sighed, loosening her necktie and slumping against the doors. "Should buy us some time, for now. This is the last place the governor'll come knockin'."

"Thank you, Tirol!" said the blue Immie, joyfully shaking her hand. "I knew we could count on you!"

However, the red Immie was less impressed. "The hell was that excuse?!" he bellowed. "Don't you have any shame? If you were my daughter, I'd be cryin'! If you wanna sell your body, then whatever, but don't assume *I* would!"

"Oh, clam it, hedgehog-head! I just saved your asses!"

"H-hedgehog-head…?!"

"Oh, that's a good one!" said the blue Immie. "Tirol, mind if I use it?"

"We're here. Come on, you two, get a move on!"

Before the argument got out of hand, Tirol slipped out of the elevator like a spy on a mission and led the pair back to her room before gently closing the door behind her.

* * *

Terrifying Steelcrab Finally Brought to Its Knees!

One more feather in the cap of the fearsome beauty Pawoo
Earlier this week at dawn, just north of the city, the Imihama Vigilante Corps succeeded in capturing a giant crab responsible for untold destruction and menacing the citizenry.

The specimen in question is known to the terrorists as "Actagawa," and they revere it as a divine beast. It is thought that its capture will deal a significant psychological blow to these enemies of the state.

Reached for comment, Governor Kurokawa, the greatest mind in all of Japan, said, "King Kong versus Big Crab… Sounds like a snoozefest to me."

Captain Pawoo did not respond to a request for comment. (*Imihama News*)

Editorial: How to Spot a Mushroom Keeper Before It's Too Late, page 3.
The comic strip "Li'l Akaboshi" is on hiatus due to the health of the author.

"So this is why y'all came here?" asked Tirol, lowering the newspaper as she sat cross-legged in the center of her room. "Listen, I ain't calling you boys stupid, but don't ya think this is obviously a trap?"

"Yes, we know," said Milo.

"Actagawa's our friend," added Bisco. "We can't just freakin' leave him."

Now in just their suits, their masks removed, Bisco and Milo flung themselves onto a fancy sofa at one end of the room.

"Oh my god," said Milo. "It's so comfy. The cushions are pulling me in…"

"Get off there!" Tirol yelled. "That was expensive! You'll get your mushroom stink all over it!"

After a few moments, Tirol cooled her head and slumped down between the two boys, pointing at the photo of Actagawa included in the newspaper column.

"I might know something," she said. "A couple days ago, this big truck arrived at a weapons factory to the north. It's not much to go on, but you'll have to move fast if you're gonna save him."

"You know where it is?"

"Don't rush. Wait until nightfall; there's a guard on the graveyard shift who's weak to a little palm-greasin'. An' don't do anythin' stupid. If Pawoo gets on your case, you're as good as dead."

At the mention of Pawoo, Bisco and Milo grew serious and exchanged a concerned glance. They knew full well that Tirol was speaking the truth.

It all came back to the Rust flower abilities that Kurokawa had obtained in conjunction with her big comeback. They allowed her to enhance the effects of the puppetshroom until they completely dominated a subject's mind. Once the flowers bloomed, there was no escape. Milo had spent the past year searching for a way to free his sister, but to no avail.

"Tirol knows what she's talking about, Bisco. We should do what she says. That means no fighting Pawoo until I come up with an antidote. You got that, Bisco? No fighting. Stay. Sit!"

"I didn't say nothin'! You don't have to treat me like a damn mutt!"

Then why d'ya act like one? thought Tirol with a sigh. Just then, the TV on one wall turned on by itself.

"Huh? Did one of you do that?"

The three of them felt their eyes drawn to the static on the screen, when all of a sudden...

SPECIAL FEATURE! IMPROMPTU PRESS CONFERENCE TO ANNOUNCE A NEW WORK FROM KUROKAWA PRODUCTIONS!!

...a gaudy jingle played as large, colorful letters danced on the screen. The trio couldn't find the words to respond. As they stared on in shock, an Immie wearing a black bow tie appeared on-screen and bowed deeply.

"*Good evening, citizens of Imihama. We interrupt this night's championship wrestling program featuring Gananja Mask in his title defense match to bring you an announcement about a new film by Kurokawa Productions.*"

The Immie gestured to his side, and the camera panned over to reveal Kurokawa, wearing a dazzling dress and shawl, sitting cross-legged on a chair in the center of a wooden stage. She lowered her sunglasses and winked into the camera.

Above her head hung a heavily decorated board with the words RUST EATER REVEAL PARTY.

"…The hell??"

Despite his sworn enemy appearing before his very eyes, Bisco had been so put off by this outrageous sequence of events that he wasn't quite sure how to react.

"Kurokawa Productions is her movie company," explained Tirol. "She does a lot of these broadcasts, hypin' up her new movies and forcin' everyone and their grandma to watch 'em as part of her freaky 'Thought Cleansing Program.' She's turned the whole bureau into a film studio."

"Movies?!" said Bisco, surprised. "You mean the shit people are being forced to watch with their eyes taped open…?!"

"Yep, they're films," Tirol said. "Everyone's forced to watch her curated selection every single day. Today it was *Rambo*, *Terminator 2*, and *Roman Holiday*."

With baffled stares coming from either side of her, Tirol rested her chin on her hands and continued.

"Kurokawa says it's to instill a healthy aesthetic sensibility in the people of today. I wonder what the real reason is, though…"

"Wait, Bisco, look at that!" said Milo, cutting short Tirol's explanation as he shoved a finger toward the screen. There, standing tall beside Kurokawa, was a woman with long black hair, gripping an iron staff.

Her sleek yet powerful physique, like a panther's, was now clothed in risqué bondage wear, like some kind of showgirl. Her face was unreadable beneath the iron skullcap adorning her head, and that, along with the gleaming staff in her hand, emitted an aura of dangerous beauty.

""Pawoo?!""

"Yeah, yeah. Kurokawa made her assistant director or some crud. Though she's more like her personal muscle…"

"H-how could Kurokawa force her to dress up like that?!" Milo lamented. "It's unpardonable!"

"…Is it?" asked Bisco. "Doesn't she wear shit like that all the time?"

"Why aren't you outraged, Bisco?! That's your wife!"

Before the boys could argue further, the announcement proceeded.

"Good evening, Imihama—no, all people of the nation. I am proud to announce the beginning of a project seventeen years in the making, and the culmination of four years of careful planning: Rust-Eater.*"*

Kurokawa's pompous speech brought the trio's attention back to the screen.

"Thank you, Governor," said the presenter. *"The people have been waiting so long for this—"*

"I'm 'Director' right now. Wake up," Kurokawa chided, her eager smile turning to displeasure in an instant.

"Apologies, Director. Now, I hear the production of this film will be largely concerned with 'authenticity.' Could you explain what you mean by that? What is 'authenticity' to you?"

"Ahh, excellent question," replied Kurokawa, staring into space for a moment. *"…Erm, what was I going to say again? One moment, please."*

She turned to Pawoo and whispered something to her. Pawoo produced what looked like a script and showed it to the governor, before whispering something back. Kurokawa nodded along intently to everything that was said, then coolly recrossed her legs and cleared her throat.

"Ahem… During a climactic scene in Throne of Blood, *filmmaker Akira Kurosawa, one of Japan's greatest minds, was said to have fired real*

arrows at his lead actor. It was this uncompromising approach to authen-
ticity, I believe, that made him a household name."

"I see."

"But I was thinking… If one authentic moment can make a film a mas-
terpiece, then imagine what might happen if the whole movie was shot that
way."

Here Kurokawa paused for a moment, then chuckled in a low voice.
The mad glint in her eye caught the presenter off guard.

"Rust-Eater is going to be a big-budget phenomenon, made with
authenticity from the moment the camera starts rolling. The filming might
well take us all over Japan, and that's why I had to invade it first, you see.

Furthermore, I've endeavored to inspire a sense of artistry into the people of
this nation, so that they can act their hearts out as extras if and when the
time comes."

"What?!"

The presenter Immie, as well as all the reporters at the press conference, began clamoring noisily.

"Y-you mean to say, Director, everything you've done in Imihama over
the last year, the war…it's all been for the sake of this film?!"

"That's right."

""Whaaaat?!"

""Whaaaat?!"

Milo's and Tirol's reactions were identical to those of the people on
the screen. Only Bisco's was different. "What a freakin' dumbass," he
said.

"And as for the main draw…," continued Kurokawa. *"…Urgh, these*
reporters are getting on my nerves. Assistant Director!"

Pawoo gave a nod, then turned to the crowd and swung her staff
menacingly. Just the burst of air it gave off was enough to make the
reporters cower in fear.

"That's better," said Kurokawa. *"You haven't even heard the best part.*
Now, where was I? Oh, yes. The leading actor. Filming will begin as soon as
negotiations to secure the role are complete. I'm sure you're all just itching

*to know what kind of superstar I have in mind for a triple-A production
like this. Well, wonder no longer!"*

A drumroll played as a large board covered by a cloth was brought
out onto the stage. Kurokawa snapped her fingers, and Pawoo gave two
powerful swings of her staff, cleaving the cover into quarters and sending it flying.

Beneath it was a life-sized cutout of a heroic young man with fiery
red hair. Alongside the image, penned in bombastic brushstrokes, were
the words:

STARRING

BISCO AKABOSHI

AS

BISCO AKABOSHI

Seeing this, even Bisco could stay silent no longer. He stood up and
yelled at the screen: "What the hell?!"

*"Akira Kurosawa once said that the reason he picked Toshirou Mifune
was that 'he liked the look in his eyes,'* " explained Kurokawa. *"Well, just
look at those! Have you ever seen a set of eyes with such a wonderful sparkle? And I have it on good authority that Bisco Akaboshi has heard my
heartfelt plea and is, as we speak..."*

Kurokawa paused and grinned, revealing her sharpened teeth.

"...right here, in Imihama."

""!!""

Those words were like an electric shock that broke the two boys out
of their stupefied daze.

"If all goes well," Kurokawa continued, *"the shooting could start
tonight. I'll keep you all apprised of the schedule, so look forward to the
show."*

Then Kurokawa stood to a storm of camera flashes. She waved affa-
bly, then prodded Pawoo to do the same.

"Well, it's been a pleasure speaking to you tonight, Director," said the
presenter. *"Thank you very much for—"*

"Oh, and one other thing," said Kurokawa, interrupting him. *"If you'll
allow me to make a little aside."*

She turned to the camera. *"If you want to see that crab of yours alive, then you won't want to wait until tonight. I've just given my orders to that weapons factory, so you'd better move quickly."*

Her pitch-black eyes gleamed behind her dark glasses.

"We'll meet again soon, hero. I'm looking forward to it."

Kurokawa flicked the camera lens, which cracked, reverting the broadcast to static snow and a drone of white noise.

�♊☉⚛ 2

"On the chime, the time will be…nine…PM…exactly."
Tick…tick…tick…BONG.

With the ring of the bell, a chill wind blew, causing a green-colored Immie security guard to shiver.

"He's late… I'm freezin' my ass off out here."

The Immie placed a cigarette through the mask's mouth (it was made to open and close) and to his lips. After skillfully taking a drag, he dropped the cigarette on the ground and stamped it out, before gazing helplessly up at the dark sky.

"Suddenly callin' me out for a shift on Friday night… City of Love, my ass. This whole town can go suck it."

"Heyyy, I'm back!"

"There you are."

All of a sudden, another Immie, yellow and slightly shorter, came running over, flapping their arms.

"You took your time," said the first. "Did you have enough money?"

"I'm sorry," said the second. "They were all out of your usual. Completely, utterly out! But don't worry: I picked one that'll blow your brains out!"

Is that a good thing…?

"Man, I'm starving! Aren't you hungry, too? Let's sit over there and eat."

The green-colored Immie took his junior's advice and sat down against the front gate of the weapons factory, placing the bag of piping-hot food between them. Whether the taste would "blow his brains out" remained to be seen, but the smell wafting from the bag really tickled the green Immie's nose.

"Here's your coffee, sir."

"Oh, thanks. So what'd you get?"

"Feast your eyes on these, sir! Hippo rice balls, hippo sashimi, hippo-tail stew, a Big Hip and fries..."

"Is there anything here *besides* hippo meat?! You're trying to ruin my stomach!!"

"Oh, quit talking like an old man. Just try it. They're running a promo now with the takeover of Gunma. They've got access to new stock, much better than the old stuff!"

"Really...?"

The guard Immie gave his junior a suspicious glance and picked up one of the synthetic rice balls, eyeing it carefully. It didn't have the characteristic stench of low-quality hippo meat, and instead smelled quite tasty.

"Right then."

""Bon appeti—""

Crashhh!!

Just as the two were about to stuff their cheeks, the factory gate behind them shook violently, launching them forward. The food in their hands fell to the ground.

"Aaah! My rice ball!!"

"Get up, idiot! Shit, the gate!!"

Crash! Crash! Crash! Crash!

With each sound, the metal of the gate warped out from the inside, before finally, on the sixth...

Ker-ashhh!!

""W-waaaaagh?!""

The doors were flung from their hinges and catapulted high into the sky, but not before catching and tearing off the younger Immie's rabbit ears. The doors then sailed through the air and came crashing down on a research facility some distance away. White smoke billowed into the air from the landing site.

"That was damn close... I thought we were dead..."

"S-s-s-s-s-sir! Look!"

The guardsman Immie slowly looked up to see an enormous crab, its orange carapace gleaming in the emergency lights.

Ka-bang!!

Freed from its restraints, it swung its greatclaw, angrily toppling a wall that read WEAPONS FACTORY #3.

And then, from atop its back came a voice.

"The hell are you two doin', sleepin' on the job? Get outta the way unless you wanna die!"

The emerald glint in the speaker's eyes shone through the darkness.

"It...it's the Man-Eating Redcap, Akaboshi!!"

Indeed, atop his noble steed sat none other than that famous villain, wanted throughout the nation.

"You're a free crab now, Actagawa!" he cried. "Ride on!"

"Eeeek!"

The earth shook as the giant crab scuttled ahead. The green Immie leaped sideways, grabbing the yellow one, who was pinned to the spot in fear, and pulling him into a decorative planter beside the gate.

Next to the fearsome Akaboshi rode his partner, Milo Nekoyanagi, the Man-Eating Panda. "I'm sorry for interrupting your lunch break!!" he shouted back.

"S-sir...," said the shorter Immie, now caked in soil, as they passed.

"What?"

"Do you think we'll get workers' comp for this?"

"You got some brass ones, kid."

The two of them watched as the giant crab rode off into the night.

"Well, that was easy. I didn't have to fire a single arrow. I thought we were walkin' into a trap."

Imihama's industrial belt was awash with searchlights and droning sirens. Actagawa hopped across factory roofs, leaving a trail of toppled chimney stacks and water tanks in his wake.

"Yeah," said Milo as they landed on the highway. "Something's not right. Given that creepy invitation, I figured Kurokawa would have done something to stop us!"

"We ain't done yet—I can smell it." Bisco frowned. "Knowin' Kurokawa, she's got somethin' hidden up her—"

Flash!!

Suddenly, a searchlight illuminated the three fugitives.

"Nicely done, Akaboshi, nicely done!"

The source of the beam, a large aircraft, slowly made its way out from behind a building with a low drone.

"Got it all on camera, in a single take!"

"Speak of the freakin' devil!" yelled Bisco, squinting into the spotlight. "What even is that thing? Looks like a giant flying starfish!"

"Watch out, Bisco! That's one of Matoba's newest models, the Dacarabia!"

The Dacarabia was an enormous flying machine that took the form of a spinning, five-pointed star. It was created using starfish bred for their size and rigged up with cameras, lights, microphones, and everything else needed for filming. It was frighteningly agile, tuned to perfection so as not to miss a single shot.

"The stillness of the night is shattered as the giant crab breaks down the walls of its confines! And atop its back..."

Kurokawa herself sat in a metal cabin suspended from the starfish's center, bellowing into a megaphone.

"...Bisco Akaboshi, a new generation of hero! Phew-ee! The audience'll love it!"

"Dammit, Kurokawa, what are you after?!" barked Bisco, his voice like a thunderclap as he spurred Actagawa on. "If you wanna fight, let's fight! Why we gotta do this bullshit every time?"

"Akaboshi. Weren't you listening to my broadcast?" said Kurokawa, before turning to micromanage the cameraman Immie by her side.

"*...Hey, lower the shot,*" she said, then turned back. "*All I want is to create the world's greatest work of cinema...starring you.*"

"A movie?!"

"*This might come as some surprise, but my dream has always been to capture a great hero on film.*"

This revelation actually *did* come as a surprise to the two boys, who froze in shock.

"*The moment you shot me through the heart, erasing me from this world...*"

Kurokawa continued speaking in soft, amorous tones.

"*...I knew. I knew you were the hero I sought. So I made up my mind—I would make you a star. It was tough after that, you know. Coming back to life, finding employment at that prison, and bowing down to that silly little flower girl...*"

"Bisco, watch out! She's trying to distract us!"

"Yeah, I know! We ain't got time to listen to your crap, lady!"

Before Kurokawa could launch into her painfully contrived spiel, Bisco passed the reins to his partner and drew the bow from his back.

"You talk big for someone who's supposed to be dead, Kurokawa. Allow me to finish what the Reaper started!"

"*Ohh, here comes Akaboshi's big scene! Don't miss a second of it!*"

Shwf!

Bisco's arrow hurtled through the night like a thunderbolt. But just centimeters from the governor's nose...

Bwonggg!!

...the sweeping, half-circle motion of an iron staff knocked it clean out of the air. The arrow fell to earth, where it exploded at one end of the factory, covering the area in red oyster mushrooms that glowed faintly in the night.

"*Hoo-ee! Your arrows never fail to put the fear of god in me! ...Hey, step in sooner next time.*"

"Yes, Director."

"Bisco, look!" said Milo.

The two boys cast their gazes to the familiar figure standing beside

Kurokawa on the edge of the cabin, her sleek dark hair fluttering in the wind.

"Bisco Akaboshi! Milo Nekoyanagi!" she roared, pointing the tip of her staff toward the moving crab. "Your insolent behavior toward the director cannot be ignored. I shall spare your life for the sake of this production, but know that not a single one of your arrows shall harm anyone aboard this craft!"

"What...?!" growled Bisco.

"Listen to me, husband. You should be proud to have been selected for this opportunity; do not shirk your duties!"

"The hell?! What's more important to you? Your family or your job?!"

That's rich, coming from you! thought Milo, as he skillfully maneuvered Actagawa through the factory district. They were now approaching the Imihama northwest gate leading to Niigata, and it was starting to concern the two boys that Kurokawa had not yet tried to attack them even once.

"*All right, scene one, 'Escape from Imihama'—that's a wrap!*" said Kurokawa, peering over a script in her hands and nibbling on the end of a ballpoint pen. "*Not bad, I must say. Now, let's move to the next location. Scene two takes place on Kobiwashi Island, off the coast of Niigata. We need to head over and make sure the place is ready, so take your time getting there.*"

"Are you crazy?! You think we'll go there just 'cause you told us to?!"

"*Oh, but you will. You know what's there, don't you?*"

Suddenly, Milo seemed to realize something. "The *sporko*! Kobiwashi Island is where all the Hokkaido Mushroom Keepers are! Chaika, Cavillacan, and the others!"

"*It's a good thing Nekoyanagi's here. It seems Akaboshi's too stupid to follow the plot by himself. Yes, in precisely forty-eight hours, I will fire our newest Ganesha gun at the island. Wait until you see the punch it packs this time. There won't be a single blade of grass left standing.*"

"What...?!"

"*If somebody doesn't save them, the very last of the sporko will go extinct... What a tragic tale. Is there no hero willing to stand up for these poor, oppressed minorities?!*"

Bisco clenched his teeth and glowered at Kurokawa with all his might. His jade-green eyes twinkled like flames, reflected in the governor's glimmering shades. Her blood racing with excitement and fear, she wrapped her arms around herself, staring directly back into Bisco's eyes as though to say, "Now I've got you."

"...*Those eyes. Those are the eyes I've been waiting for, Akaboshi! This isn't a game. I would do anything to bring out your full potential... Do you remember what kind of person I am?*"

"You're a sick bastard!"

"*Not anymore. I'm a sick lady now. Toodles.*"

Kurokawa snapped her fingers, and the Dacarabia began to spin, giving rise to a great storming gale, like a tornado. The two boys raised their arms to shield their eyes as their cloaks flapped madly in the wind, and the flying machine took off in the direction of Niigata.

"...The conquest of Imihama. It was all for the sake of this film..."

Milo thought back to what Kurokawa had said on the TV broadcast last night.

Could it really be true? She's doing all this for a movie?

Milo thought back to what he knew of the governor. This new female Kurokawa seemed even more unhinged than the old one.

"No time to mope, Milo. We gotta get over to that island."

"So we can save the *sporko*, you mean?"

"I don't know what Kurokawa's deal is, but I can tell she's serious. She looked me right in the eye. That means she's stronger than when she was a guy, at least."

Milo nodded and took the reins. Then something occurred to him.

"Bisco," he said. "Why don't we split up? One of us can go get help."

"Help?" asked Bisco. "From who?"

"You know who! He's helped us before! I'm sure he'll be glad to—"

"Stop. Don't say any more, Milo."

Bisco narrowed his eyes. Without turning to look at his partner, he continued.

"I can't rely on my old man to break us out of every jam. We'll do it ourselves. Me and you—his student and mine. I wanna give him somethin' nice to take with him when he passes on, and this might be our last chance."

When Bisco finished speaking, Milo nodded, and placed his hand over his partner's.

"I get it. Shall we go, then?"

"You bet your ass."

"All right. Ride on, Actagawa!!"

The two boys and the giant crab dashed off in the direction of Kurokawa's aircraft, moving through the black of the Imihama nightscape, with the usual fire back in their eyes.

龠⽊⽬◉⽊⽊ **3**

"Hyo-ho-ho! So high up! The buildings look like ants!"

"Splendid, isn't it? This canyon is one of our most popular desti-nations... But I must warn you to keep away from the edge, sir. The winds get awfully cold up here."

"Don't treat me like some old man, sonny!"

Earthmirror Gorge, in the northern reaches of Yamagata Prefecture, possessed a peculiar soil that was filled with tiny gemstones, caus-ing the earth to glisten in the sunlight. This made it one of the most famous natural heritage sites in all of Japan.

However, few tourists were willing to brave the treacherous roads to Yamagata, and the land was too barren to use for farming, so the Yamagata government was at a loss for how to capitalize on this natural wonder.

That was where the Yamagata Air Force came in. A few enterprising pilots with time to spare roused their freeloader escargot planes and started up a small skydiving venture over the valley. The sight of the sparkling colors as one parachuted through the air was something to behold, and word quickly spread until the business had the official sup-port of the Yamagata treasury.

"Ha-ha! What a magnificent sight! It wasn't cheap comin' up here, but I'm glad I did!"

"We're so happy to hear that, sir. Now we're coming up to the drop point, so—"

"Can't wait. I wanna drop now!"

"What?!"

As the old man approached the plane's open side door, the staff hurried to stop him.

"W-wait a minute, sir! You're not even wearing your parachute!"

"What's that, sonny? That old thing ain't gonna save me! When it's time, it's time!"

"S-somebody help! Hold him down!"

"Grrrrgh! Get...off...meeee!"

A total of three staff members barely managed to fit him with his diving suit and parachute, after which the old man grumbled, "Bah. This old junk's just gonna weigh me down."

"Phew! What an energetic gentleman. Now, we'll jump on three. Are you ready?"

"Ready!"

"That's what I like to hear! Three..."

"Hup!"

The old man immediately leaped into the wind, his white whiskers flapping.

"Two— Wait, whaaat?! I can't *believe* this customer!"

The startled diving assistant quickly hopped off the plane in pursuit. The elderly gentleman screamed a lively "Wahoo!" as his white ponytail fluttered behind him.

"Please don't hurt yourself, sir!" called the assistant, diving after him. "I'll get fired!"

"What a bother," the old man grumbled. "Can't you stay outta my way when I'm havin' fun?"

"I have to make sure you're okay..."

"Escargot to Dive Leader Hirasaki, please respond. We have a problem."

"I know! I'm trying, but he won't listen!"

"Not him! We're picking up weapons on the radar. Something in the clouds ahead. Something... Whoa, what is that?!"

This concerning message caused Hirasaki to turn and look back at his plane, just in time to see a bolt of lightning rush out from a cloud and pierce the escargot's belly. The engine exploded, and the blast wave caused Hirasaki to lose control, tumbling through the air.

"Oh my god!" Hirasaki wailed, as a stray piece of wreckage cracked his goggles. "An escargot plane, destroyed? That's never happened before!"

Just then, a broken-off wing sailed through the air toward him.

"W-waaaah?!"

He threw his arms over his face, knowing full well it would do nothing to protect him. Just then…

Fwip! Fwip!

…two arrows flew past him, skimming his ears before landing in the wreckage and exploding with a *Gaboom! Gaboom!* into two clusters of white mushrooms that tore the wing apart, saving Hirasaki by the skin of his teeth.

" Wh-what happened? Mushrooms?!"

"Hyo-ho-ho-ho! Clever of you to include this little surprise for me!"

"O-old man! You're a Mushroom Keeper?!"

Hirasaki turned to see the elderly gentleman with a bow in his hands, firing shot after shot with untraceable speed and astonishing power. A rapid succession of arrows flew past the soldier once more.

Gaboom! Gaboom! Gaboom!

Debris rained down incessantly on the pair, but the old man blew every last piece away with his arrows and mushroom arts. Once the sky was clear again, he casually put away his bow.

"Now, to enjoy the rest of my flight!" he quipped.

"You're amazing, sir! What's your name? You must be famous!"

"Pipe down, sonny, and mind yer own business! Now, tell me how to use this parachute thingamabob. That's what I paid you for, ain't it?"

"O-okay!"

The bewildered diving instructor did as he was told and guided the elderly gentleman to the designated drop point.

The night air was still, the heavens illuminated only by countless stars. A gentle pillar of smoke rose from a tent erected at the top of the gorge, where a pot was simmering over an open fire. The old man dipped his wooden spoon into the bubbling ocher stew and brought it to his lips.

"Mmm. Mmm. Fwoo!"

His reaction failed to make clear whether he enjoyed the taste. To the unsuspecting, he was just a happy old man, but those who sensed the true power lurking beneath the surface could see him for who he truly was: Jabi, hero of the Mushroom Keepers.

"Hyo-ho-ho! This skydiving lark ain't as bad as I thought! Just wait until the old hag hears about this!"

Jabi dipped his spoon once more into the mysterious stew (which, according to him, consisted of rat meat and hen-of-the-woods mushroom soup) and slurped it up ravenously, before pulling out a notebook from somewhere on his person. He made a large tick on the page and glanced over the remainder—a written list.

"...Skydiving...check. Not many left now! Maybe I've been a bit overzealous. Wonder if I should add a few more for good measure?"

He scratched his head for a few moments, when all of a sudden, he heard a noise.

"Hmm?!"

Outside the tent, a few rocks and boulders broke away from the cliffs and tumbled into the gorge. Jabi had set up truffle incense to ward away insects, so anything that approached the tent was most likely a dangerous predator.

"Who's fool enough to disturb my mealtime?" he grumbled. "Show a little respect."

Jabi picked up his bow and exited the tent. At the same time, he cleared his mind and extended his senses for any turbulence on the still surface of the pool that was the world around him. The technique was called "*Soulprinting*." Banryouji monks studied for years to learn it, but Jabi had just kind of figured it out by himself, and for him, executing it was as simple a task as breathing.

...Hmm? That's odd. I ain't pickin' up a darn thing. False alarm?

"H-help me!"

"Hyo-ho?"

Just as he was about to give up and head back inside the tent, Jabi heard a staticky voice coming from behind him.

"I—I can't hold on! I'm fallin', I'm fallin'!"

"Well, I'll be! Busy day for savin' lives!"

Jabi tottered over to the cliff edge, where he spotted a strange robotic jellyfish, painted bright pink, hanging from the brink.

"What in the blazes?!"

"G-Gramps! It's me, Tirol! You gotta help me!"

"Goodness, lassie! You gone and replaced your body with some sort of mechanical contraption? Even I ain't that kooky! What a waste of a pretty gal!"

"Y-ya think? Eh-heh-heh... Wait, no, ya old coot! This ain't me—it's a remote-controlled drone! I came to talk to ya; ya gotta pull me up!"

"Come to talk to an old man like me? So kind of you, lassie. Let's get you up, then!"

Jabi lowered his bow and allowed the dangling Tirol drone to grab on to it, before flinging her back onto solid ground. The drone cried out, retracted its arms, and turned into a ball, rolling across the ground and into Jabi's tent.

"Oops. Guess I don't know my own strength."

There was a clang and a shout, and Jabi zipped back inside the tent to see that the Tirol drone had knocked into the pot of stew, spilling the contents all over itself and the floor.

"Oh, what have you done, girl? That was supposed to be my supper!"

"That was your fault, old man!" yelled the drone, stripping the pot from its head and casting it aside. *"Seriously, like son, like father! You both gotta be a little gentler with these things!"*

"So what is it you wanted to tell me, lass?" said Jabi, whipping out his pipe and taking a few careful puffs. "...Actually, on second thought, I don't wanna hear it. Just leave me be."

"It's about Bisco! He's in huge danger!"

Tirol's own face appeared on the large display attached to the drone's head, as her static-laden voice came through the speakers.

"His wife's been taken hostage, and the sporko *are all gonna die! Milo and Akaboshi are trapped, with no choice but to do what Kurokawa says!"*

"…"

"The thing is, Kurokawa's totally fixated on him! She won't be expectin' an attack from outside! But the Kusabira and the Benibishi are busy with their own problems, so…"

"So you want me to stage an attack on Kurokawa, that it?"

"Yeah! You're the only one we can count on! It was hard to track ya down, I gotta say, but now I've found ya! And there ain't no way Kurokawa'll be ready for your legendary skills!"

"I ain't doin' it."

"Whaaat?!"

"I said, I ain't doin' it."

Tirol was taken aback. Before she could respond, Jabi reached into his pocket and pulled out the notebook from earlier.

"Wh-what's this?" Tirol asked as the drone's camera zoomed in on the cover. There, in whimsical lettering, were the words AKEMI HEBIKAWA'S BUCKET LIST.

"…Akemi Hebikawa?"

"Jabi's just a nickname. That there's my real name. Oh, the girls used to go wild for old Akemi… You can call me that, too, if'n you like."

"Like hell I will, ya senile old fart!"

"Reckon I'll be dead by the end of the month…"

"Listen up, Gramps! Those boys of yours are in trouble! Are ya gonna let a little thing like dea—? Wait, what?!"

"Really pulled out all the stops back in Tokyo, ya see. By rights, I should be dead already. It's only 'cause of this Bishamon concoction that I'm still kickin'."

"Y-you can't be serious…"

"But I'm tired o' cheatin' death, lassie. Reckon I'm about ready to lay these bones to rest. Bisco's all grown-up now; he don't need an old man like me to look out fer him no more. I'm gonna do the things I wanna do, and then I'll be on my way."

At Jabi's urging, Tirol turned the pages of the notebook and peered inside.

AKEMI'S BUCKET LIST
- GET A DHARMA NAME
- KILL A PIPE SNAKE BY MYSELF
- MAKE OUT WITH A WIDOW
- DOODLE ON THE OLD HAG'S FACE
- FINISH ALL VOLUMES OF KARIAGE-KUN

...

"..."
"What? There's more on the next page, y'know. Take a gander."
"*No, It's fine. I got the gist of it...*"
Tirol's voice took on a grave tone, and she handed the notebook back. Then, not quite knowing what to say, she fumbled with her words for a while.
"*...Bisco would blow a fuse if he knew I'd come to talk to ya today,*" she said at last. "*And I know I don't have the right to tell you how to live what's left of your life. But...*"
"..."
Jabi patiently awaited Tirol's next words with a smile on his face.
"*But...that's why you gotta go see Akaboshi one last time. He's still just a kid...and you're his hero, y'know? He'd never forgive himself if he wasn't by your side at the end...*"
Jabi was silent for a moment, then he exhaled a puff of smoke and asked, "You sure you're the real Tirol, lassie?"
"*What?! You don't trust me?!*"
"Hyo-ho-ho! Just a joke, lass. Your earnest words threw me for a loop, that's all."
With his peaceful smile, Jabi looked ready to ascend to heaven that very moment. Tirol could say nothing to change his mind, so she stood the drone up and made to leave the tent.

"...*See you, old man. Or maybe I won't. Have a good death...I guess. Is that what they say?*"

"Never heard you sound so considerate, lassie. Tell Bisco he's an idiot for me, will ya?"

"*Sure. Good-bye...*"

Then the Tirol drone retracted into a ball and rolled away. Jabi watched it go and took another puff of his pipe.

"*Hmm... Bisco, eh?*"

A childish grin crossed his lips as something occurred to him. At the bottom of the list, right under *Skydiving*, Jabi scrawled another entry.

"*Namari interceptor craft synchronization rate at ninety percent.*"

"*All systems nominal. Both main engines and all four sub-engines ready.*"

"*Mantra reactor link secure. Ready for takeoff.*"

The fleet of Milo Primes uttered their final reports. The hangar doors opened, and out came Actagawa, his claws raised triumphantly in the air, with several gleaming flight attachments equipped to his carapace. His two masters sat atop him.

"*Bravo!*" came a voice. "*I'm seeing—*Cough!*—a twelve hundred percent power gain over the average steelcrab specimen!*"

"Is that a good thing, Professor Namari?"

"Shut up, Milo! We ain't got time to listen to his explanations! We'll be here all day!"

The two boys were fastened into their upgraded saddles with seat belts. Namari's excited voice came through a speaker in their headrests.

"*Listen, boys. This flight system draws its power from the mind of the crab that pilots it. That means that Actagawa there will be the one in control.* Cough! *Simply put, if he wants to be free of it, he will. From here on out, it'll all be about the bonds of trust between you!*"

"Hmph. Same as always, then," grumbled Bisco. Something obviously upset him about the whole arrangement. As he traced his finger along his tattoo, he asked the gods for forgiveness.

* * *

Bisco and Milo hadn't been sure how they would reach Kobiwashi Island before the end of Kurokawa's two-day time limit. This was where Tirol, the brains of the party, came in. She suggested reusing the Actagawa jet boosters from back when she helped the boys inside Hokkaido. However, Tirol was currently busy acting as a double agent for Kurokawa, and couldn't lend a hand with the engineering, so the boys were left with only one choice: to seek out Professor Namari, the figure who had originally assisted Tirol with this technological leap in crustacean aviation.

And so it was that the boys came to Niigata, which as of now was still narrowly outside Kurokawa's control, to find the reclusive engineer and secure his assistance.

"Whoa! Doesn't this just get your heart racing, Bisco?!"

"Like hell! The only thing making my heart race is what the gods are gonna do to us for makin' crabs fly!"

Below them, Rocket Actagawa, his joints clad in engines, stamped his legs onto the catapult rail with an enthusiasm his brother very much lacked.

"*This is it, boys! You're going to do what Mother Nature could not!* Cough! *You—no, we—no, I! I shall be the one to pull this lever, and herald in a new age! A new age of decapodan evoluuutionnn!*"

"E-erm… Professor?"

"Oh crap, all the blood's gone to his head."

"*Are you ready, boys?! Oh yes, you are!! All hands, prepare for takeoff!*"

In the control room, Namari was so flushed, his face was practically steaming. The more his blood boiled, the more blood seemed to drain from the two boys' faces.

"P-Professor!" Milo yelled. "Perhaps we should…calm down and—"

"*Let's go!! Disengage safeties!*"

The Milo Primes all ducked for cover as Actagawa's main engines began to roar, blue sparks dancing within them. Actagawa trembled with anticipation and raised his greatclaw high overhead.

"W-w-wait, wait!" protested Bisco. "W-we don't actually need to go that fast…"

"Give my regards to Kobiwashi Island, boys!!"

Namari pulled the takeoff lever, and the catapult rails sent Actagawa hurtling down the launch corridor at breakneck speed, flinging him out over the vast ocean. However, Actagawa's back boosters had yet to ignite, and the giant crab simply sailed through the air toward the water's surface.

"W-waaaagh?! Wh-what are you doing, Actagawa?! Fly, fly!!"

"We're gonna crash!!"

Actagawa pitched forward like a large plush doll. Then, just as he was about to hit the sea, his eyes twinkled.

Roooaaaaarr!!

The engines ignited, and blue flames erupted from their rear, kicking up a spray of seawater. Actagawa went speeding forward and upward like a rocket, spinning in the air as though unsure what to do with all his excess energy. It was lucky the two boys were strapped into their seats. Otherwise, they surely would have been flung from their saddles.

"Waaaaaagh!" screamed Milo, as though his delicate throat would tear. Bisco, meanwhile, clapped both hands over his mouth and tried his hardest not to throw up. Actagawa paid no mind whatsoever to the two boys, setting his thrusters to full throttle and jetting off in the direction of Kobiwashi Island.

* * *

"Are you all right, Bisco? Do you need another shot for the nausea?"

"…Urp. I'm fine… I think Actagawa's calmed down, too."

Thirty minutes after launch, Bisco and Milo were flying over Kakudahama Bay. Actagawa had grown used to his newfound movement capabilities, no longer overeager to loop and twirl in the air at the expense of his passengers.

"We'll make it in plenty of time at this rate!" said Milo. "All thanks to Tirol and Professor Namari!"

"I get we're in a hurry, but have you thought about how we're gonna get back?" asked Bisco.

"Professor Namari included a collapsible cargo hold," Milo explained. "It'll be a tight squeeze, but we should be able to fit all the *sporko* in there, and then carry it behind us with Actagawa."

"I don't like this," Bisco grumbled, his crimson hair flapping in the wind. "There's no way an engineer like Namari has flown under Kurokawa's radar. That lab might've already been under her control."

"I guess. So?"

"So?! We could be flyin' a mechanical death trap!!"

Milo laughed, his aqua hair blending in with the sky. "Well, it's not like we can do anything about it. We can't start doubting everyone, Bisco; that's what Kurokawa wants. Let's just— Wah! Bisco! Look at that!!"

Milo tensed and stared straight ahead. Following his gaze, Bisco could see a towering cumulonimbus cloud, and in front of it, a swarm of winged scorpions heading straight for them.

"Seagull-eaters," said Bisco, drawing his bow. "Not a threat on their own, but in those kinda numbers..."

"What should we do, Bisco? Shall I cast a mantra?"

"No need. A quick burst of numbshroom spores oughtta do the trick," said Bisco, attaching an arrow to the string and drawing it back. "You just keep your hands on the reins, and—"

Before Bisco could finish, a loud *Bzamm!* heralded the appearance of a mysterious bolt of lightning. It snaked through the air before striking one of the seagull-eaters, and with a *Bzzzt!* the creature's carapace was scorched black. Its four dragonfly-like wings tattered and torn, it spiraled helplessly out of the air, landing with a *Plop!* in the ocean.

"What the hell? Lightning?!"

"Actagawa, watch out!"

Milo pulled on the reins, causing Actagawa to veer to the side, narrowly avoiding a bolt heading straight for him. The lightning skimmed the steelcrab's underbelly and hit a seagull-eater behind him. It then darted between the creatures one after another, sending them all to a watery grave.

"It's aiming for the scorpions… Bisco! This is no ordinary lightning!"

"It's comin' from that big-ass cloud!" shouted Bisco, lowering his cat-eye goggles. "I'm pickin' up heat from inside it. There's something livin' in there!"

"Correct, Akaboshi!"

They could hear a wicked voice from within, amplified by a megaphone. Then a starfish-shaped flying machine burst out, splitting the cloud like cotton candy.

"I was hoping to delay that reveal a little longer. Oh well. I couldn't exactly let those scorpions interfere with your big scene."

"Kurokawa!"

"Thought I smelled somethin' rotten."

"I see you two are raring to go. That's good. Personally, I've been too stressed over the shoot to get much sleep lately. Anyway, it's time for me to explain scene two."

Inside the cabin, Kurokawa adjusted the newsboy cap—a directorial cliché—on her head as she brushed her other hand through her pine-needle hair.

"Since time immemorial," she bellowed through her megaphone, *"car chases have been an absolute must in any action movie. Take* Die Hard *or* Mission: Impossible. *Whatever you watch, there's bound to be a chase in there somewhere. Now, I don't really get the appeal, but this is an action movie, so we have to put one in… But here's the thing: There're almost no highways suitable for car chases anymore, and barely any cars to drive on them. Plus, you guys don't even have driver's licenses!"*

"Where are you going with this, Kurokawa?!"

"That's when I had an idea. Instead of a car chase, why not a dogfight over a vast expanse of ocean?"

Kurokawa pointed at the orange meteor that was Actagawa and whistled gleefully.

"And to fight your flying crab, I came up with this! The Cumulo 5! We tested its power en route, and it brought down an escargot plane with a single blow. Will our brave heroes outlast its fearsome lightning and reach the

island to save the sporko?! *This is a lot more exciting than watching some dumb old cars play tag on the ground, don't you think, Akaboshi?!"*

"Do you have to flap your gums every time we meet?!"

Bisco loosed a mushroom arrow, but once again that glimmering staff appeared and knocked it prematurely out of the sky with a *Bwonggg!!* Pawoo stood atop the Dacarabia, her long raven hair streaming in the wind.

"I told you, your arrows are futile! Brute force will get you nowhere, my love!"

"You're one to talk!"

"Lights! Camera!"

Kurokawa bellowed into the megaphone, and the Immie cameramen aboard the craft all pointed their cameras toward Actagawa. The Cumulo 5 rumbled ominously, purple bolts running like snakes all across its volume.

"Aaaction!"

Kurokawa swung her megaphone, and lightning shot out of the cloud toward Actagawa. Milo cried out, "Bisco, get down!" and pulled the reins, sending the rocket-propelled crab into a nosedive. This evaded the first bolt, but the cloud expelled a second, and a third, relentlessly bearing down on the trio.

"We have to fight back," said Milo. "But where do we even begin?! How are we supposed to fight a cloud?!"

"The goggles're tellin' me it's some kind of giant basket star," said Bisco.

"Basket star?! You mean those wiggly starfish things with all the feelers?"

"Yep. Dunno how they got one to fly, though."

Deep-sea creatures such as basket stars and anemones were often used as animal weapons, owing to their simple brains and strong life force. However, nobody had ever made one that flew around in a cloud and shot lightning. It only went to show the depths of Kurokawa's insanity that she was prepared to funnel enormous amounts of cash into the production of such a beast just for the sake of a movie.

"But if it produces heat, I can see it. And if I can see it, I can hit it!"

Once Actagawa was steady, Bisco nocked three arrows to his bow and fired them into the cloud. The arrows all stuck into one of the feelers of the Cumulo 5 just as the beast was gathering power for its next attack. A moment later, there was a series of *Gabooms!* from inside the cloud, and a cluster of red oyster mushrooms burst out.

"All right!" cheered Milo. "You hit it!"

"Bravo! Marvel at Akaboshi's skills, everyone! Hey, you better be getting this on camera!"

"Dammit, I can't take this anymore!"

Keeping a careful eye on the Dacarabia as it circled Actagawa, Bisco took a deep breath and focused on the dormant Rust-Eater spores within him. As the power awoke, his body began to sparkle with a golden light.

"I'm done entertainin'!" he said. "Let's see them try to film this!"

"You have a plan, Bisco?"

"That cloud, there's one part that's darker than the rest. Can you get us there?"

"Leave it to me!"

Amid the fluffy white was one region that crackled with ominous lightning. Aided by his goggles, Bisco could see that was where the body of the Cumulo 5 lurked. Milo lashed the reins and drove Actagawa right into it.

"Uh-oh. Are they going to defeat it already? That's no good; that thing cost me a fortune. If they end things too quickly, it'll screw up the pacing!"

"Allow me to prevent that, Director."

"Don't be ridiculous! The director's assistant doesn't get a cameo!"

Actagawa wove between bolts, deflecting others with his greatclaw, before eventually arriving right at the beast's belly.

"Take the shot, Bisco!"

"All right!"

Bisco exhaled, drawing an arrow so bright, it gave off a crimson halo.

"Take this!!"

Pchewww!!

A red light streaked through the sky, faster than the eye could follow, piercing the dark cloud and striking the creature's core. The Cumulo 5 rumbled, its body writhed, and it began launching bolts of lightning everywhere.

"Got it!"

"...No, Bisco! It's still alive!"

There was a *Bzzzam!* as a stray bolt flickered toward Bisco, and...

"Deploy shields!"

...Milo's cube immediately shrouded the pair in a force field, narrowly deflecting the blow. However, another bolt came for Actagawa the moment Milo's hands were off the reins, and managed to strike the crab in the stomach.

"Aaagh!! Actagawa!!"

Actagawa lost control and fell into a tailspin, smoke spewing from his engines.

"What the hell?!" cried Bisco. "The Rust-Eaters didn't grow!"

"Stay with me, Actagawa! I'm sorry, but this'll sting!"

Milo rummaged around in his medical bag for a bright-red syringe, then thrust it into Actagawa's joints between sections of armored carapace. Actagawa fell toward the ocean, but just as he was about to hit the surface...

Fwoosh!

...the giant crab regained consciousness in the nick of time, reigniting his boosters and jetting back up into the sky. The two boys clung to the reins for dear life, before letting out a sigh of relief once their rocket-powered steed was safely back in the air.

"We were almost shark bait," said Bisco. "Milo, what did you do?"

"I used the Bishamon compound to bring him around," Milo explained. "Actagawa's bad with lightning, remember! One more hit like that, and we're dead!"

"I thought I dealt the killin' blow," grumbled Bisco. "Did I miss or somethin'?"

Meanwhile, a huge chunk of flesh fell from the cloud. Still in midair, a host of Rust-Eater mushrooms burst to life across it. The limb then continued falling and hit the ocean with an enormous splash.

"…I see," said Milo. "There wasn't anything wrong with your arrow, Bisco. The basket star used its lightning to cut off the infected limb before the mycelium could spread!"

"Wh-what?!"

"If this drags on, it'll have the upper hand. We need to stop it from using that lightning," Milo said, deep in thought, with one hand pressed to his head.

"Wh-whoa! Milo! Look out!" cried Bisco, snatching the reins from him and dodging the incoming blows. Just as Bisco was about to throw up from all the ducking and weaving, Milo hit upon an idea.

"I've got it!" he said. "We've just got to make the clouds go away! There can't be any thunder if there are no clouds!"

"Make them go away?! Who do you think you are? Amaterasu?! We can't control the weather!"

"Yes, we can! I learned how at school!"

Milo fished through his quiver for several identical-looking arrows and passed them to Bisco. Then he lifted one hand in front of his face and began chanting. The next moment, all the Rust particles in the air swirled and gathered in his palm, coalescing into an emerald cube of mantra power.

"What're these?" asked Bisco. "Heatwave arrows? What am I meant to do with them?!"

"I'll explain later!" Milo shot back. "For now, just fire them on my mark!"

Milo flew Actagawa around the Cumulo 5, dodging its attacks while suspending cubes of Rust in the air. On Milo's command, Bisco fired at them, hitting each and every one with peerless bowmanship, turning them into spherical red mushrooms.

Heatwave mushrooms, as the name suggested, took advantage of nucleosporous fusion to produce radiant heat. They were very useful to the nomadic Mushroom Keepers, who used them as portable heaters.

However, they were also very dangerous, with the potential to spiral out of control if handled incorrectly. When loosed weakly, they gave off only a paltry warmth, but if fired from a strong bow, they could easily burn down a tent by mistake.

And if fired by Bisco, the greatest bowman in the world, they could even make the cool autumn air feel like it was the height of summer.

"Wh-what a scorcher!! What's that Nekoyanagi kid up to?!"

Kurokawa and her film team were starting to feel the heat.

"D-Director! Th-the tripod's getting hot! Ow, it's burning my hands!"

"Quit whining! Our lead's out there risking his neck for this film, and so should you! You'll keep those cameras rolling even if the flesh melts off your bones!"

Kurokawa puffed out her sweat-slick chest and began wafting herself with a large fan.

Meanwhile, a veritable minefield was taking shape around the cloud, the red mushrooms pulsing and floating as if they were at sea.

"That's right! Looking good, Bisco!" Milo said.

"Tell me what the point is already! Don't say you're tryin' to steam us all to death!"

"Do you know how clouds are made, Bisco? Allow me to explain."

"Um, what?!"

Milo went on, all the while dodging incoming bolts of lightning.

"When air rises and expands, it cools, causing all the water vapor you usually can't see to condense out of the air and form tiny particles of water. That's what clouds are made of! So that means—"

"All right, I get it, I get it! Just tell me the point already, Professor Smartass!"

"The point is...!"

Milo muttered one last mantra to the cube in his hands and clicked his fingers. When he did, all the cubes on which the heatwave mushrooms were growing suddenly grew spikes of Rust, impaling the mushrooms and causing them to explode. An incredible rush of temperature caused a wave to form on the ocean, expanding outward from the blast. Bisco closed his eyes in an attempt to withstand the heat. And when he opened them again…

"…What?! The cloud's gone!"

"Right?"

Indeed, the cover that once cloaked the Cumulo 5 like a big ball of cotton wool was nowhere to be seen. Lightning crackled along its tentacles, but it was unable to muster up a single thunderbolt without the charge dispersing into thin air.

"Ruuuuuugh!"

The basket star wiggled and coiled, bereft of its weapons and armor. Milo looked at it and smiled, his sweat-drenched brow glistening.

"See that?!" he yelled. "That's the power of education!"

"Don't get cocky," spat Bisco. "This ain't over yet."

"Oh, come on! Can't you say, 'Well done' or 'That's amazing'?!"

The Cumulo 5 lashed out with its complex, overlapping appendages, but against Actagawa, this was a fool's struggle. Aided by his rockets, he swung and slashed, tearing the creature apart and dropping severed limbs into the ocean.

"Looks like Actagawa's been itchin' for some payback," said Bisco. "Milo! Do your thing!"

"Got it!"

Bisco took over the reins, and Milo placed his hand on Actagawa's giant claw, chanting his usual weapon-creation mantra.

"Won/shad/viviki/snew!!"

Crystalline Rust covered Actagawa's claw. It gleamed in the cloudless sun as he stretched it out ahead like an emerald spear.

"Look, it's their finishing move! Make sure you get it on film!"

"S-sorry, Director, we're just changing the reels…"

"What?! Get on with it! Sometime before we all die of old age, please!"

Paying no mind to the argument on the Dacarabia behind him, Actagawa fired his main thrusters and shot toward the center of his foe.

""Go for it, Actagawaaa!!""

Thud! His claw sank deep into the creature's core.

"Ruuugh…"

Then, with fearsome strength, he sliced upward.

Slash!

"Ruuuuuughhh!"

A cascade of green blood poured from the resulting gash. Actagawa turned his back on his foe, then swished his claw to fling off the creature's guts. The emerald coating, its job now complete, glinted and dissipated into dust. The Cumulo 5, now unable to sustain its buoyancy, slowly but surely began plummeting into the ocean.

"We did it! Good job, Actagawa!"

"It'd be a lot more satisfyin' without that asshole grinnin' at us."

Bisco glowered at Kurokawa, who was still in the Dacarabia's cabin. She was beaming proudly, having caught everything from the finishing blow to Actagawa's victory pose on her beloved camera.

"Excellent work, Akaboshi! This is exactly what I was after! What kind of car can take down a giant floating weapon and top it all off with a cool pose? This is just another element that sets my film apart from history's finest... Huh?!"

Kurokawa's gloating was interrupted when a device went off in her pocket.

"What is it?! Don't you know we're filming?! ...Huh? The Ganesha gun? Oh! Power it down. We've got all the necessary footage, so there's no need to— What?! You fired it?!"

A stir went through Kurokawa's team members, Pawoo included. Kurokawa grabbed the phone from where it was wedged between her shoulder and her ear, her tone growing agitated.

"What the hell do you think you're doing?! I said not to fire until twelve! ...It's twelve now?! You idiot! I meant midnight! Midnight!!"

Bisco and Milo watched them from off in the distance.

"What's going on?" asked Milo. "They seem to be arguing about something..."

"Why don't we just shoot her now? Even Pawoo's not payin' attention."

Soon, however, Kurokawa grabbed the megaphone and started shouting.

"Er… Sorry for the holdup, Akaboshi. I was going to call off the attack, since you won, but there's been a little mix-up."

"A mix-up?"

"Turns out the Ganesha gun's already been fired. Just now. Whoopsie!"

Kurokawa tipped her head and assumed the cutesiest pose she could muster, but the wildfire in Bisco's eyes caused her to stand back at attention.

"Erk! W-well, you know what they say! No use crying over fired artillery! There's bound to be a few mishaps on set! Let's just bring this energy into the next scene, and—"

"Bisco, look!" Milo yelled, cutting off Kurokawa. Rising from the continent in a ballistic trajectory was what looked like a giant cannon-ball moving at incredible speed.

"Agh! The shell from the Ganesha gun! We'd better make ourselves scarce before it blows!"

"That's it," said Bisco, his eyes trained on the target like a hawk, analyzing its trajectory. "It's gonna sail right over us and score a direct hit on the island."

"What do we do, Bisco? Do you think the Mantra Bow can…?"

"No need. We got the perfect weapon to stop that thing, right here!!"

Bisco flashed his partner a cheeky grin and pulled a good old-fashioned anchor arrow from his hip. First, he ordered Actagawa to turn. Then he aimed his bow at the still-falling remains of the Cumulo 5.

"Bisco, you're not serious!"

"Time for a little pole fishing! Help me out, Actagawa!"

Bisco fired his arrow, which landed in the core of the Cumulo 5. Its enormous bulk was far too heavy for a normal human to lift, but with Bisco's monstrous strength, it was like hauling cotton.

"Rrrrrrrggghhhhhhh!"

"B-Bisco! That's amazing!"

Actagawa supported Bisco by firing his rocket boosters, and as soon as the deadly projectile was straight overhead…

"Rrrraaaaaagh!!"

…Bisco hoisted the legendary catch into the air, where it was perfectly timed to collide with the oncoming artillery shell, resulting in an enormous explosion.

""Waaaaagh!!""

"*Whoaaaa?!*"

Neither Actagawa nor the Dacarabia could escape the powerful blast wave, and both were knocked clean out of the sky. Moments before hitting the sea, Actagawa rolled level, weaving left and right to dodge the chunks of basket star meat raining down from above. Seafood shower thus averted, Actagawa fired his boosters, setting a course straight for Kobiwashi Island.

"...Zzz... Zzz... Hnguk..."

The autumn wind jostled some paper scraps, carrying them up to tickle the nose of a brawny-looking, bearded *sporko* keeping watch over the vast ocean.

"...Grott, been sleepin' 'gain. Better pull in some fish else the women-folk'll tear me head off."

This particular *sporko*, it seemed, had a habit of blurting out his every thought when no one was around to hear. He clambered down from the watchtower and walked out into the shallows, digging through the sand until he found the tip of his net.

"Not that I 'spect to find more than a few grottin' bleakfish, mind. We 'ad it all in Hokkaido: tuna, skipjack, eel... What I'd nae give for that kind o' grub 'gain."

The bearded *sporko* gripped his net and, with a heaving yell, hauled it as hard as he could.

"...Whit?!"

The fisherman was surprised to find the net much weightier than he'd expected. He could feel something large caught in it, twisting and trying to escape.

"Wh-whit a catch! We'll be feastin' tonight, fer sure!"

The *sporko* pulled out a bone horn and blew into it, letting its tone ring across the island. In a few short moments, more *sporko* appeared from the forest.

"*Ouya!*"

"What's happening?"

"It came from the beach! Get over there! *Ouya!*"

They flocked to the struggling fisherman, each bearing the tools of the work they had just been doing.

"We got a reight big one in the net!" the bearded one explained. "It'll be enough fer a feast tonight, I kid ye nae!"

"*Ouya!* You don't say!"

"Hey, everyone! Get down here and give Induk a hand!"

About a dozen *sporko* grabbed the net and began heaving, but even their combined might could not draw the mysterious catch inland.

"Grott, 'e's a feisty bleighter! He'll tear the net to shreds at this rate!"

"Induk! Ey heard ye horn and came a-runnin'!"

"Aye! Grab the net and let's— E-Elder?!"

Induk turned to see the latest helper was none other than Cavillacan himself, a polar bear of a man with legs like tree trunks.

"Gyah-ha-ha! Te fish givin' ye trouble, young'un? Slack nae, the Ghost Hail gods be watchin' over ye!"

"I—I ken, Elder, bit we be dealin' wit a real monster here! It don't wanna budge!"

"Hrm..."

The other *sporko* could see Cavillacan working up his rippling muscles even from under his thick wool coat. He squatted, and then...

"Yaaaah!!"

...with incredible speed and force, he snatched the net and hoisted it clean out of the ocean, causing the water to rush like a tidal wave. The dark silhouette of the catch loomed overhead.

"*O-ouya!* What strength!"

"Cavillacan, son of Hokkaido, strongest in all the land!"

The other *sporko* rejoiced as Cavillacan approached the beached catch and eyed it suspiciously.

"Hrmmm...??"

"Great Elder, just look at the size of this thing! The whole tribe'll be eating crab leg stew tonight!"

"Hold on… Jest where've I seen this crab before…?"

"Take care, Elder… I fear that thing be still kickin'…"

Cavillacan ignored Induk's warning and approached, when suddenly he noticed the two saddles atop the giant crab, and the two unconscious boys sitting in them.

"Grete balles o' fire!!"

"E-Elder?!"

"Akaboshi! This be Akaboshi's crab! An' the boye's still reidin' it!" He turned to Induk, agitated. "They meight've swallowed te sea. Tek 'em te the village te see Chaika!"

"Grott! Akaboshi, in me net, of all places?!"

"*Ouya!* Carry him back! Quickly!"

The *sporko* clambered onto Actagawa and unfastened the two drooping boys, causing a great commotion as they carried them back to the group's makeshift village.

* * *

"…

"G…

"Gblaaagh!"

From out of Bisco's mouth came a long, narrow eel, covered in his gastric juices but still alive.

"Bisco! Milo, Bisco's awake!"

"Chaika! Stay away from that!"

The eel's skin glowed a pale, eerie shade of blue, and it leaped for Chaika's open mouth. Milo snatched it out of the air in the nick of time and crushed it in his fist, a display of brutality very much not in keeping with the good doctor's looks.

"Eek! Th-that was frightening!" exclaimed Chaika. "What was it?"

"That was a Stomach Eel," said Milo. "They go inside people and devour them from within; it's horrible… I guess Bisco's guts were a little too tough for it."

"You know, the more I hear about you, the less I think you two are even human…"

"*Koff.* Quit talkin' shit and help me out. I'm dyin' over here."

Bisco cleared his throat of any remaining mucus, then took a look at his surroundings.

"Where am I?" he asked. "I remember flyin' away from an explosion on Actagawa, and then…I don't really remember. What happened? We need to go save Chaika and the others!"

"Who do you think just saved you?"

"Huh?!"

Bisco looked down and was met with the adorable gaze of the oracle he had rescued only one year prior.

"What the—?! You're Chaika! The hell are you doin' here?!"

"What do you mean?! This is our home! You're the ones who came crashing in uninvited!"

"I didn't recognize her at first, either," offered Milo in an attempt to back up his partner. "The *sporko* all wore such thick coats before. Look at her now; she's like a fashion model!"

Chaika proudly puffed out her chest in agreement. While she still wore her trademark hat, the girl had ditched her coat in favor of a midriff-baring crop top, making the difference in her islander genes plain to see. Puberty had hit her like a storm and granted her a figure the envy of any modest young Japanese lady, while her fair skin and shimmering golden hair all contributed to the northern princess's majesty.

"Well, I couldn't keep wearing that stuffy old thing," she said. "It's so hot down here, I can't believe it's only fall. How do you people live like this? No wonder you all act like barbarians; it's the heat getting to your heads!"

"Chaika!" said Milo. "That's no way to speak! It's only Bisco who acts like a barbarian!"

"Way to throw me under the crab, asshole!"

"Anyway!" said Chaika, changing the subject. "Poor Actagawa is recovering under our care. He's so dizzy now he can't even walk straight. Honestly, I can't believe you two. Actagawa's such a sweet little thing, and you two have been driving him around like a pair of madmen!"

"Hey!" Bisco protested. "We came all the way across the sea to save your asses, and—!"

"That's not the point! What's the good of all your mushroom powers if you can't even keep one little crab safe! If you're his big brother, then start acting like it!"

The oracle's scolding was like a punch to his gut. Bisco wasn't normally one to sit and listen to somebody complain after he'd just saved their life, but Chaika's words struck a chord with him, and soon he and Milo both found themselves sitting meekly in repentance.

"...Hmph! It's good to see you two know how to listen! Very well, that's all. Do better next time!"

Chaika took their hands and helped them to their feet, a beaming smile across her face.

"If I know the pair of you, I know just how hard you must have been fighting for our sake. As oracle, I must treat our saviors. Tonight will be a feast! We may not be able to offer you the same hospitality we could in Hokkaido, but for tonight, you can forget all your worries and cares!"

"Lookit her, Akaboshi... Me Chaika... Leike a wee angel, she be..."

"Don't know any angels who talk like her."

"We *sporko* 'ave bit one hope...that our daughters meet wit strong husbands... She's me only daughter, Akaboshi..."

"Aw, hell! Why's everyone I meet always pawnin' their kids off on me! I'm a married man, dammit!!"

Several of the *sporko* came over, saying to their elder things like, "C'mon, you're drunk!" and "You're making our guest feel uncomfortable!" but Cavillacan was already so far gone that he refused to listen to them.

"Well, somebody's popular," said Milo, stuffing a whole fish skewer into his mouth and side-eyeing Bisco from across the table.

A cluster of women noticed the doctor boy's dashing good looks and exchanged giggle-filled whispers, before picking themselves up and trotting over, intending to fill the seats around him. However, just before they could reach him...

"Milo! Looks like my father is giving Bisco a hard time, wouldn't you say?"

Chaika stepped in front of the women and shot them a harsh look. The girls sulked and sat back down. There wasn't much they could say to the oracle of their village.

Chaika gently seated herself beside Milo and softly pushed her shoulder into his. However, Milo's gaze was fixed intently on his partner, and his expression didn't budge a centimeter.

"Come on!" said Chaika, annoyed. "Eyes over here! I'm the oracle of this village! You could at least blush or something!"

"Sorry, but I have to monitor Bisco," he replied.

"Monitor him?!"

Milo took the cup of white sake Chaika was offering him and downed it in a single gulp.

"There wasn't any need for this before," he explained. "Not when everyone was still scared of him. But now he's softened up."

"Isn't that a good thing?" Chaika asked. "I mean, who minds him lightening up a little?"

"I mind!!" yelled Milo, rosy-cheeked, his sapphire eyes flashing as he pointed at the cause of his distress. "Look at him! I used to be the only one who knew how cute he really was, and now everyone can't get enough of him! I have to keep an eye out so none of these overly forward *sporko* girls try to lead him astray!"

Chaika gave a deep, exasperated sigh. "You're overreacting," she said, waving her hand in front of Milo's eyes in a vain attempt to make him so much as blink. "Bisco's a hero. He saved Hokkaido. It's no wonder everyone loves him. And Father's been lonely ever since his Mushroom Keeper partner passed away... He probably just enjoys talking with him."

"...What's that? Cavillacan's flying solo now, is he? ...You don't say..."

"W-wait, Milo!"

"Just try to switch partners, hedgehog-head; I dare you. I'll poison you and then myself..."

...I let his pretty face fool me. It's the blue one I should be afraid of!

Chaika was taken aback by the handsome young man's inner darkness, but it wasn't long before the atmosphere of the party caused her to forget all about it.

The fire crackled as *sporko* musicians played relaxing folk songs on flutes of bone and lutes strung with Hokkaido's muscle fiber. The haunting melodies seemed to call back memories of the womb. It was a touching performance that Milo did not expect from the rough-and-tumble Mushroom Keepers of the north.

"...I'm glad to see the *sporko* are doing well," he said at last. "I was worried about what would become of you after you were forced out of your home."

At Chaika's insistence, Milo had sobered up a little, at least to the point where he could hold a conversation without paranoia getting the better of him.

"You were right to worry," said Chaika sadly. "Our people are not as happy as they once were."

"Really? But everyone seems to be having so much fun!"

"Before, they'd be three times merrier. You only have to listen to this melody... It's a ballad to Hokkaido, our mother. Nobody will say it, but they're worried about her."

"..."

Hokkaido had fallen.

After Mepaosha had revealed herself to be Kurokawa, she had granted the power of the Rust flower to her Neo-Immie army. The *sporko* Mushroom Keepers, Benibishi soldiers, and Kusabira devotees all teamed up to combat this threat, but even this trifecta of mushrooms, flowers, and Rust was ineffective against Kurokawa's terrifying new invention. Before long, Hokkaido was recaptured, having only just won its freedom from Shishi's camellia, and now it floated weakly in the Pacific Ocean, defeated.

"It'll be okay, Chaika," said Milo, a troubled look on his face. "Whatever Kurokawa's planning, we won't let it happen. Bisco and I will figure out the secret of her Rust flowers and save Hokkaido, I promise!"

"You don't need to promise me anything, Milo. I know you can do it!"

Chaika gently wrapped an arm around him and shot him a cheeky grin. There was no trace of the frightened little girl he and Bisco had run into so long ago inside Hokkaido.

"Actually, Chaika...I have something to ask you."

"What is it? Anything!"

"I need a sample of the Ghost Hail spores. They might be the key to unraveling this whole mystery."

Milo produced a small notebook and turned to a page of handwritten notes. Chaika took a peek, but the whole thing was covered in chemical formulas she didn't understand.

"I'm working on a vaccine, and the Ghost Hail is one of the necessary ingredients. I figured you would be able to help me... Can you?"

"That...might be difficult," Chaika admitted. "The Ghost Hail only grows in the depths of Hokkaido. It's too delicate to exist for long outside— Oh!"

Chaika's face lit up as she realized something. She reached up inside her hat and rummaged around.

"Is this it? No...that's my sweets collection... And that's where I keep my amulets..."

"How much are you hiding under there?!"

"Ah, found it! Here, take this!"

Chaika pulled out something small and white, and held it reverently out to Milo.

"What is this...? A crystal?"

In the light of the fire, it sparkled like a diamond. Its surface was as pure and unmarred as freshly fallen snow, and glittering white spores fell off it like snowflakes.

"It's crystallized Ghost Hail spores. Unlike regular spores, they won't decay."

"A Ghost Hail…crystal?!"

"It's a secret treasure of the village. I took it with me when we fled Hokkaido. I'm not supposed to show it to outsiders… But for you, Milo, I'll make an exception!"

Milo wasn't sure he could take something so precious, but it was clear in the oracle's eyes that she trusted him, and Milo wanted to live up to that trust.

"Thank you," he said. "I'll be sure to put it to good use!"

"…Tee-hee!"

"What?"

"It's just, sometimes, Milo, your eyes look just like Bisco's."

Hidden behind her golden hair, Chaika's cheeks reddened ever so slightly. In one determined gulp, she drained her cup of fermented goat's milk and gazed at Milo with dreamy eyes. There was no trace of her usual haughty attitude whatsoever.

"I already thanked Bisco…," she said. "Now it's time to thank you…"

"…Erm… Chaika? I—I think you've had a little too much to drink…"

"Sit still, Milo… That's an order."

"Time out! Time out!"

Now it was Milo's turn to deal with an overstimulated drunk. Chaika may have been an innocent girl, but she came from a long line of brawny Mushroom Keepers, and strength was in her genes. Milo looked like a deer in the headlights as Chaika held him in her unbreakable grip, slowly bringing her rosy lips closer…

"Wagh!!"

Something leaped out of the bushes nearby, only to trip on a rock seconds later and fall face-first into the dirt.

"Wh-what?!"

"Chaika! Get behind me!"

Milo recognized the threat immediately and went straight for the dagger at his belt.

"Owww… What's this damn rock doing here? You're supposed to

clear these away, Assistant! Now we've missed our chance to capture this totally organic kiss scene!"

A woman picked herself up off the ground and patted the dust from her outfit. She quickly inspected the camcorder in her hand for damage, and upon finding it intact, let out a "Phew!" and wiped her brow exaggeratedly. "Thought I'd broken it for a second there... Looks like the tape's all good, too."

"Kurokawa!"

As soon as Milo said her name, the whole party descended into chaos. From out of the bushes stepped dozens of camera-wielding Immies. Kurokawa's forces had surrounded the entire place while they were feasting.

"Finally decided to show up, huh?!"

Bisco leaped off his lavish seat of honor and into the air, tearing up the grass as he landed beside Milo.

"Never thought you'd show your face," he growled. "For a third-rate director, you sure got some guts."

"I don't suppose there's any point in asking for a retake?" Kurokawa said with a shrug. "Sorry to spoil your meal, Akaboshi. Entirely the fault of my witless staff. How about I go back into the bushes and we try this again?"

"Like hell, dumbass. You're not gettin' away this time. I'm gonna leave your precious film on the cutting-room floor!"

In the blink of an eye, Bisco readied his bow and loosed a shot at Kurokawa, but her fearless grin didn't crack as the projectile hurtled toward her.

Bwonggg!!

A raven-haired whirlwind appeared from one side, deflecting Bisco's arrow with one swing of her staff. Pawoo landed beside the governor, her lithe muscles rippling like a panther's. Then she stood up and pointed her gleaming staff at the two boys.

"That's amazing, Pawoo!" cried Milo. "You blocked Bisco's arrow at such short range!"

"This ain't the time to be impressed, dumbass!"

Bisco looked back at Pawoo, his teeth clenched and eyes gleaming. He took a deep breath, and the golden light of the Rust-Eater enshrouded his body. Kurokawa watched all this with the same unbothered grin.

"Oh? Sure you don't want to calm down a little there, Akaboshi?" she asked. "I suppose if you go all out, you *could* bore a hole straight through my little bodyguard and get to me easily."

"...!"

Seeing Bisco had understood her point, Kurokawa smiled and went on.

"She's brainwashed, you see. She'll gladly give her life for me. And you, Akaboshi... Is our hero so determined to defeat the evil villain that he'll turn his beloved wife into mushroom food?"

"...You sick bastard...!!"

Bisco paused, his bow fully drawn, his teeth clenched so hard they nearly cracked. Milo couldn't remember the last time he'd seen his partner so furious.

"It's all part of Kurokawa's game," he whispered in an attempt to pull Bisco back to his senses. "Don't fall for it!"

"I know. Dammit!"

"It's nice to see you have someone with brains on your side, Akaboshi... All I have is this gorilla woman, and she doesn't even laugh at any of my jokes."

"Don't say another word about her!" Milo scowled. "Or I'll make you regret it!"

"Oh my. Looking at the two of you gives me the willies! All right, you win. I'm leaving."

Kurokawa snapped her fingers, and the Immies all receded into the forest and disappeared. With one last wave and a "Ciao!" Kurokawa followed suit. The two boys watched them go, unable to fire a single shot.

"Oh, yes, I almost forgot," said Kurokawa, just before she was out of sight. "Our next location. Powder Mountain, in the north of Yamagata. Queen Shishi and the rest of the Benibishi are being held there. The bombing is in two days, so don't be late. I wouldn't want to see our expensive set piece destroyed..."

Traveling along the Weeping Valley to the southern reaches of Akita, one comes upon the Swaying Plains, a field of swaywheat almost three meters tall. On foot, a person could lose their way amid the long stems, but the pair sitting atop Actagawa's back encountered no such issues.

Flying close to the ground with his jet boosters, his carapace glinting orange in the sunlight, the giant crab offered a pleasurable cruise across seas of gold. It was a majestic sight, but one that the two boys were very much not at liberty to admire.

"Hmm... Got it! Now, if I could just reduce the stickiness..."

"The hell're you mutterin' to yourself back there?"

It was rare for Bisco to be holding the reins, but Milo was otherwise occupied. Somehow, he'd managed to set up his medicine-mixing machine on Actagawa's back and had spent the journey puzzling over it and, as far as Bisco was concerned, speaking complete nonsense.

"I've started to get a hold on what the Rust flower is composed of," he replied, "but I still need more time. Kurokawa's gone to great lengths to make sure I don't reverse engineer it so easily."

"But this is you we're talkin' about. You'll find a way, won't you?"

"You bet!"

The trio was moving fast, and they very quickly put the Swaying Plains behind them. Before long, a tall gray mountain loomed on the horizon.

"There it is," said Bisco. "Powder Mountain."

Powder Mountain was a rich source of redpowder, the explosive mineral that gave the peak its name. Even now, miners chipped away at the rock, selling their hauls to Matoba. It was a lucrative venture, and a month's labor could earn you enough to live on for a year. However, the mountain was also home to a powder miner's worst nightmare, the firebean: a round, bulbous insect that gorged itself on redpowder and exploded in order to scatter its grubs.

"It smells like guns," said Milo. "And it's so barren. Couldn't Kurokawa have picked a livelier spot?"

"What do we care?" Bisco grunted. "C'mon, Actagawa, let's go!"

Bisco lashed the reins, and the crab's thrusters ignited, taking the three of them up the slope of the mountain.

The apex of Powder Mountain was an ominous place, with veins of redpowder sewn into the rock like bloody scratches. But the most unsettling sight of all was the bizarre construction atop the mountain's peak.

"The hell is that?!"

Actagawa thudded into the earth, blasting away bits of rock and redpowder as he landed.

"Whoa! Bring us down gently next time, Bisco!"

Bisco was unable to spare an ear to his partner's objections due to the unbelievable sight before him. He peered through his goggles at the building's signage.

"Kurokawa's…Professional…Psycho…Thriller…House?"

The building itself was clearly hastily constructed, mostly rectangular and painted all black. The sign Bisco had read was made up in striking, gothic letters, and above it was an amateurish drawing of a cartoon Immie displaying its perpetual smile. The two boys were deeply unimpressed with the craftsmanship on display.

"…"

They dismounted, walked up to the building, and stared at it with blank looks. Beside what appeared to be the main entrance was a tacked-on notice at a wonky angle that read:

Greenroom for Mr. Akaboshi & Mr. Nekoyanagi

"Oh boy! I wonder if they made us lunch."

"Like hell they have, dumbass!"

Bisco smacked his partner on the back of the head and scowled at the waiting door.

"How stupid does she think we are? I'll level this whole place from the outside with one shot!"

"You can't do that, Bisco! What if—?"

"—*The hostages are inside? That would be the obvious conclusion, wouldn't it, Akaboshi?*"

From a speaker high up on the wall came Kurokawa's voice.

"*I know you're smarter than this, Akaboshi, and I intend to prove it. In this scene, we'll be seeing the ferocious Man-Eating Redcap's clever side.*"

"Kurokawa!!"

"*Apologies for the mess. I know it looks cheap, but it was the best I could do on short notice. No need to worry; I assure you the inside is done up much better. Besides, Saw didn't have any exterior shots, did it?*"

"That bastard…always hidin' somewhere my arrows can't reach!"

Bisco scowled and ground his teeth in anger. Milo looked at him. Then, after a moment, he pinched his partner's cheek. Hard.

"Owww! The hell'd you do that for?!"

"Calm down, Bisco. C'mon, let's go," he said, striding through the front door.

"Y-you're just walkin' right in?!" asked Bisco with astonishment as he hurried after his partner. "Ain't this an obvious trap?!"

"If Kurokawa wanted to kill us, she'd have done it already," Milo replied, no trace of worry on his face. "Besides, by following your instincts, you're doing exactly what she wants. We'll never find an opening that way. What we need to do is make her doubt herself, and the fastest way to do that is to follow her instructions exactly."

"…"

"That way, she'll start thinking, 'What does he know that I don't?' If she's going to slip up, that'll be when she does it."

"…Yeah, that's what I was thinking, too. I was just testin' you."

"Whatever you say."

"You callin' me a liar?!"

"Oh? Akaboshi, I see you're not your usual rebellious self today. Yes, that's right, come inside. Wait in your room here until everything's ready... Hey, somebody get our actors some refreshments! ... What's that? Giraffe brains? You idiot, we can't serve them that mush! You're fired!"

Listening to Kurokawa's lively exchange on the other side of the speaker system, the two boys followed the marked path deeper into the mysterious building.

The bare light bulbs dangling from the low ceiling were so hot they roasted the dust in the air, filling the narrow corridors with a burning scent. The walls were unpainted concrete with bare wiring, and it was clear no effort had been put into looks back here, either.

"Owww!!"

"Bisco?! What's the matter?"

"I hit one of the light bulbs... Shit, I think it burned me. What's wrong with this place?! Spare a thought for the stagehands, won't ya?!"

"It left a mark on your forehead. I'll put some cream on it later... Oh, isn't this the place?"

Milo pointed to a door that read GREENROOM FOR MR. AKABOSHI & MR. NEKOYANAGI. It was the only thing in sight that looked halfway decent.

"...I don't like this," said Bisco. "Watch out—there could be spore gas or anythin' in there."

"Coming through!"

"Waaagh!! What are you, a five-year-old?!"

With no concern for his partner's fears, Milo turned the doorknob and marched into the room.

"Oh, it's quite big in here... Looks okay to me, Bisco. Come on in!"

How the hell ain't he freakin' out?

Bisco accepted Milo's point that against Kurokawa, jumping at shadows was a sure path to defeat, but Milo's degree of carefree abandon was almost unimaginable. Bisco didn't know whether he should be impressed or worried.

"There's a dresser, a makeup stand... Do you think I should cover up my panda mark?"

"What the hell's up with this room...?"

Bisco crept in, still determined not to let down his guard. It was a stark contrast to the halls outside, with all sorts of creature comforts like air-conditioning, a humidifier, and even a full-length mirror.

On the table in the center of the room were plastic bottles containing refreshments such as Flamebound tea, gilded elephant tea, orange juice, grape Fanta, and even a powerful pick-me-up called Firesnake Drink.

"Hmm, none of 'em seem poisoned..."

"Bisco, look at this! They even made us lunch boxes!!"

Still in awe of his partner's childlike glee, Bisco wandered over and followed Milo's starry-eyed gaze. There on a table in one corner of the room sat two lunch boxes. The one labeled MR. NEKOYANAGI looked exceedingly expensive, made of several lacquer containers bundled in fancy wrapping paper and tied with a golden string.

"Look, Bisco, a golden lunch box! These are hard to get!"

"Never even heard of it. What's inside?"

"Give me a second... W-wow!!"

Milo loosened the string and lifted the lid off the first box. It was still warm, and released a heavenly scent that filled the two boys' nostrils.

"It's royal salamander! This would cost you over one thousand sols at a restaurant!"

"Wh-what?!" exclaimed Bisco, looking over at the sleek salamander flesh adorning a bed of brown rice. Ever since becoming apprenticed to Jabi, Bisco had been obliged to put up with his master's strange tastes, and for a long time, he hadn't known what it was like to genuinely enjoy a meal. It was one of the many pleasures he'd only learned after journeying with Milo.

"You don't see food like this every day! Let's eat it together, Bisco!"

"F-fine, I guess... Can't fire a bow on an empty stomach."

"Oh? It looks like yours is different from mine."

Bisco looked down once more and found his own lunch box. Upon closer examination, the only part resembling Milo's was the label saying MR. AKABOSHI. Alongside it was a small rectangular card with these words, written in powerful strokes:

FROM YOUR WIFE.

"...From Pawoo?"

Puzzled, Bisco flipped over the card to find a hastily scrawled message on the back.

> *Dear Akaboshi,*
>
> *I was hoping to cook you a magnificent meal to help you reach your full potential today. Unfortunately, your wife rather brusquely told me to stay off her turf, so I'm afraid you're eating gorilla chow instead. My, you should have seen her. Even the brainwashing couldn't make her change her mind! Oh well, they do say the quickest way to a man's heart is through his stomach. Though personally, I have my doubts...*
> *See you onstage in thirty minutes.*
>
> *Director Kenji Kurokawa*

"P-Pawoo made this?!"

"Whaaaat?! Bisco, you have to open it! Quickly!"

"Like hell! What if there's a bomb inside?"

"There's not! Pawoo would never do that!!"

Faced with Milo's wide-eyed eagerness, Bisco reluctantly popped open the lid and took a look inside.

"...Ooh?"

"Wow! Way to go, Pawoo! This looks amazing!"

In the lower box were three smallish rice balls, while the upper box was full of all sorts of colorful side dishes, with great care apparent in their placement. The star of the show was grilled sea urchin, alongside green peppers wrapped in dolphin bacon. It was garnished with toasted tomatoes, lentil-and-*senju* potato curry, and fried baby iguana

tails, a lineup guaranteed to seize the heart of any meat-loving man. There was even a small dessert in the corner: white mochi with orange juice drizzle, a loving present from a wife to her darling husband.

"Hmmmm."

Milo, however, was even more interested in the lunch box than its recipient was, scrutinizing the contents carefully before finally giving it a thumbs-up. "Perfect score!" he practically yelled.

"Whoooa! Don't spit all over it!" shouted Bisco.

"Pawoo's never been a great cook," Milo went on. "It's her love that inspired her to make all this. Aren't you lucky to have a wife like her? Or rather, a friend like me to introduce you...?"

"All right, all right! Let's just eat already. The note said we only got thirty minutes!"

The two sat themselves down excitedly and got to work. The moment Milo placed the salamander meat on his tongue, its juices filled his mouth with a savory taste.

"Mmmm!"

"Grrr..."

"You want some, too, Bisco? Here, open wide!"

"Piss off! Mine's just fine!"

Bisco turned back to his own meal in a huff and tried one of Pawoo's offerings.

The taste was nothing to write home about, but every part of the meal was made with care and consideration. This didn't go unnoticed by Bisco, trained as he was in the art of perceiving his opponents' intentions. Granted, that usually occurred in the context of a battle, and not at lunchtime, but the theory was the same.

"Listen, Milo," he said. "Your salamander might be tasty, but that's all it is. This meal has purpose. The secrets of her nonlethal staff techniques are hidden within it."

"What?! In the food?!"

"Yeah. Take this rice ball, for example..."

Bisco picked up one of the appetizers and popped it into his mouth. "Ggh?!"

"B-Bisco?!"

With a complete disregard for etiquette, Bisco pulled the half-eaten piece of food back out. Miraculously, it was the same shape as when it had gone in.

"Wh-what's the matter? Was there too much salt?"

"It's…"

"It's…?"

"It's hard as a damn rock!!"

Bisco's best guess was that the woman's unnatural strength was to blame. When molding them, she must have pressed so hard the ingredients compressed, like carbon into diamonds, with an equivalent effect on the human teeth that dared to bite into them.

Milo picked one up in his hands. "It's like metal…," he said. "I knew something wasn't right; Pawoo's attempts at cooking have always been doomed to failure. Don't worry; leave the rice balls and just have the meat. You can share some of my—"

"No. I'll eat it. Pawoo worked her ass off to make this."

"Wh-whaaat?! A-all of it?!"

"She put her blood, sweat, and tears into this meal, so I gotta do the same, even if it kills me! Now, hand that back so I can—!"

"Hello, boys! Hope you haven't been waiting too long!"

Just as Bisco fought to steal back his lunch, a familiar voice echoed over the greenroom's speakers.

"Sorry about that. It took a little while, but we're ready to start shooting! I'm afraid I'll have to ask you to cut your lunch break short and come over here immediately."

"We're still eatin' here!" Bisco yelled back at the speaker. "Can't you push back the filmin' instead?!"

"Heh-heh-heh. Oh, by all means, continue your lunch if you wish, Akaboshi…"

The governor's voice grew dark and ominous.

"But know that the clock is already ticking. Do you really wish to sit around sipping tea while the poor queen's head is split open like a tomato?"

"Hurry, Bisco!"

"Is she in here?!"

Bisco kicked down a door at the end of the hallway, revealing a pristine white room completely unlike the previous corridors. It was small and plain, and in its center, behind a thick sheet of tempered glass, were the Benibishi children, huddled and cowering.

"What does Kurokawa want with them…?"

Milo didn't have to ponder this for long. Soon, a voice came in over a hidden speaker.

"Get ready! It's time to begin scene three!"

The voice took the two boys by surprise, and they instantly prepared for trouble.

"Now, we got to see a lot of your crab in scenes one and two, but we can't drown the audience in action scenes—it's time for a little suspense. You ever seen the movie Cube? I'll lend you a copy sometime."

"I've had it up to here with your yappin'!" yelled Bisco. "Just say what you want us to do already!"

"Wonderful! It's so good to see you getting into character!"

Her voice laced with excitement, Kurokawa launched into an explanation.

"Let's start with a little warm-up, shall we? Beyond the glass in front of you, as you can hopefully see, are a bunch of innocent Benibishi children.

Oh, just look at their lovely skin! I bet you can't keep your eyes off them, can you?"

"What are you goin' to do to them?!"

"See the timer up top? You have three minutes. When that timer reaches zero..."

Kurokawa left a dramatic pause, punctuated with chuckles.

"...I'll fill the room with my patented Wither Gas, and all those poor little children will die."

"Kurokawa!!"

"Assuming you wish to prevent that, you'll have to take my special quiz. Answer all questions correctly, and I'll stop the countdown... Uh-oh! Not so fast, Akaboshi! Touch your bow, and I'll set off the gas immediately!"

"That sick freak...!!"

Presently, an Immie came in pushing a small portable table and gave a sharp bow to the two boys.

"The hell's this??"

"Now, let me explain... Hmm, where was it? Page forty-five? No..."

The sound of flicking pages came over the speakers as the timer continued ticking down.

"Hurry the fuck up!" Bisco yelled.

"Sorry, sorry, sorry! Okay... Ahem. I'm only going to explain this once. The rules are as follows: You should see two buttons, one red, one blue. One will stop the gas, while the other will release it immediately. Only the Immie in front of you knows which is which. This Immie is either a lying Immie, who always lies, or a truth-telling Immie, who always tells the truth. The problem is, lying Immies and truth-telling Immies look completely identical in every way. You may ask this Immie one, and only one, yes-or-no question! Which singular question can you ask that will allow you to press the correct button and save the children?!"

Milo furrowed his brow and pondered the problem deeply. Then he noticed Bisco looking calm as a summer's day.

"You seem confident," he said. "Have you worked it out already?"

"I think so," replied Bisco. "But no, that can't be it. It seems too easy…"

"Wow, I'm amazed! So what's the answer?"

"It's a fifty-fifty guess," he explained, rushing over to the buttons. "We've been coastin' through on one percent chances this whole time, so this is like a godsend."

"Whoa, whoa, whoa! Stop!"

"*Stoppp!!*"

Bisco's bold solution terrified Milo and Kurokawa both. Milo raced over and grabbed his partner around the waist, pulling him back.

"*What kind of scene would that be, Akaboshi? Play the game seriously! I'm adding a new rule: Press the buttons randomly, and you lose!*"

"I *am* bein' serious!"

"It looks like we can't rely on brute force, Bisco. We have to play Kurokawa's game and solve the riddle…"

"Then let's take that bunny guy's mask off! One look at his eyes'll tell me whether he's lyin' or not!"

"*That's not how you solve a riddle! You have to use logic! No instincts or gut feelings allowed!*"

With yet another of his "brilliant" ideas shot down, Bisco crossed his arms and grumbled, struggling to come up with anything else. Milo, however, now that his partner was prevented from doing anything drastic, turned his thoughts inward, fishing for a solution in the sea of his inner knowledge.

"Only one question… Hmm…"

"This is dumb," protested Bisco. "It doesn't matter what question we ask. We don't know if he's lyin' or tellin' the truth!"

"…"

"Dammit! We're runnin' outta time! Let's just press one of 'em, Milo!"

"No! I've got it! It doesn't matter whether or not he's lying!"

Milo's sapphire eyes glimmered, and he turned to the Immie and posed his question.

"If I were to ask you, 'Does the blue button turn off the gas?' would you answer 'Yes'?"

"…???"

Bisco couldn't make head nor tail of Milo's interrogation. The Immie remained silent for a few seconds, before raising a sign in his left hand that read No.

"It's the red button, Bisco!"

Trusting his partner's words, Bisco immediately leaped to the buttons, pressing the red one. The two boys turned their eyes toward the timer on the far wall. It had stopped with only two seconds to spare.

"Countdown aborted," came a computerized voice. *"Shutting off gas."*

Behind the glass, the Benibishi children cheered and hugged one another.

"I don't get it," said Bisco, wearing a puzzled frown. "How did you know if he was tellin' the truth? Was it just a guess? If so, that was my idea."

"No! I did it properly, unlike you!"

Milo pointed an accusatory finger and launched into his explanation.

"I still don't know if he was a truth-telling Immie or a lying Immie, but it doesn't matter. With my question, even if he was lying, he would have answered truthfully."

"H-huh??"

"Basically…"

"Nekoyanagi's question would have caused the Immie to lie twice," interrupted Kurokawa, sounding extremely satisfied. *"If there's only two answers, then a lie about a lie is the truth. And the truth of a truth is also the truth. Oh, I knew I could put my faith in you. The good doctor of Imihama never fails to disappoint."*

"…Huh???"

"It's okay, Bisco. You don't need to understand it…," said Milo.

"Anyway, excellent work clearing the demo round! Oh, and by the way, if you hadn't found the correct solution, then either button would have caused you to lose."

"What?! That ain't fair!"

"Show them to the next floor, if you please."

The Immie nodded and led the pair out a door to the next level of the building. Bisco picked up his pace and caught up to the suited goon.

"So tell me," he said. "Were you a liar in the end or what?"

"A truth-teller," was the Immie's curt reply. With this new information, Bisco pondered the puzzle once more, before shaking his head and forgetting all about it.

U-urgh...

Shishi groaned inwardly as her mind dragged her back into consciousness. Shaking her head to dispel the fog, she found it oddly heavy, and from the touch of steel on her forehead and neck, she surmised she was wearing some sort of metal torture helmet.

Wh-what have they done to me?!

She was strapped to a chair, with belts around her legs, and both hands handcuffed behind her back. About the only thing she could move unrestricted was her neck.

I've been tied up! she thought. *What a disgrace, for me to become a prisoner once more!*

The terror of waking up to find oneself a hostage in some unknown location would be overwhelming for most people, but Shishi's will was strong.

...Do not panic, she repeated to herself. *Do not be angry! They have left you alive, and that hubris shall be their undoing. You are king now, and a king always finds a way out. Now think: What would Father do?*

Shishi had suffered far worse than this at the hands of the merciless vice-wardens of Six Realms. Her mind was therefore unperturbed as she pondered a means of escape.

Impressive-looking manacles. But the mechanism is quite simple.

Before her eyes was a glass pane, but there was no guard in sight. *How fortuitous,* Shishi thought, as she focused on her wrists, and pollen danced in the air around her.

Come on, reach! I beg of you!

Dark ivy snaked up her wrists, painfully slow, and crawled into the keyhole.

Yes! I still have enough Florescence!

The mask around her head was made of steel and protected by three thick locks, but like the handcuffs, their construction was simple. Shi-shi concentrated, extending her vines, and soon they reached the inside of the first lock.

Okay, nearly there…

But just as she was about to pick it, her father's knowing eyes flashed in her mind.

…This is too easy. What's going on?

She was up against Mepaosha, who previously had not only Sataha-baki, but all of Six Realms wrapped around her little finger. Plus, she now bore the power of the Rust flower, whose might young Shishi knew only too well. How could she possibly have thought such flimsy restraints would hold her prisoner?

…No. I mustn't hesitate, or I'll lose my chance! Flourish!

A *Bwoom!* came from inside the lock, and a bright-red camellia blew it open. Just then…

Crkcrkcrkcrk!!

Rrgh?!

…an electric current issued from the torture mask and made her whole body go stiff.

"Urgh… Aaaaagh!!"

Shishi curled backward until her spine creaked as she screamed her throat raw. The electricity was enough to burn her vines black, and they crumbled to ash.

"Now, welcome to the next room— What's going on in here?! Oh, that silly child! Cut the electricity, quick! You'll kill her! Oh dear…"

From somewhere far off, she heard Kurokawa's panicked voice. Just as she was about to pass out, she heard a *Ker-lunk!* and the electricity stopped. Shishi went limp and collapsed in her chair, steam rising off her body, her crimson eyes hollow. From time to time, her body emit-ted a little spasm.

Suddenly, someone kicked down the door and came in, yelling at the speaker.

"Shishi!! Damn you, Kurokawa!!"

"Who set the shock collar to lethal?! I said to leave it on punish! She could have died!"

Shishi could smell her own scorched blood, but she managed to raise her head toward the familiar voice and smile.

"B-Broth...er...!"

""Shishi!""

Bisco and Milo ran up to the glass barrier separating them from Shishi. Milo stared into her eyes, then sighed in relief.

"Phew, she's okay! This isn't fair, Kurokawa! You haven't even told us what we're supposed to do yet!!"

"She tried to escape! ...Which I predicted, but unfortunately, some fool set the output on the shock collar too high. Rest assured, the individual responsible has been fired. Hey, it turned out all right, didn't it? Don't get so angry. Besides..."

A spotlight inside the room illuminated the suffering Shishi.

"...now you know what will happen should you fail."

"G-grrr...!!"

Shishi bit her lip, filled with regret.

I was too naive!

She had followed right along with Mepaosha's script, humiliating herself while Bisco was watching. From between her barely open eyelids came a single tear that dripped down her cheek and into her lap. Milo couldn't bear to watch, and his eyes glowed with rage.

"Oh, don't give me that look, my dear Panda. You'll get me all excited. Now! On to the next game! Ta-daa!"

The two boys watched in confusion as an Immie with a towel over his shoulder entered the room and placed some sort of game on the table, before bowing and taking his leave.

"Wh-what's this?" asked Bisco. "Wait, I've seen this before!"

"Ah yes, a game so famous, even our resident barbarian has heard of it! Correct! Your next challenge will be to play this game of Pop-Up Tyrant!"

"...Pop-Up Tyrant?"

"Watch closely, if you please."

Upon the table was an old children's game with which Bisco and the other amusement-loving Mushroom Keepers were deeply familiar. The centerpiece was a plastic barrel with slots for swords, containing a miniature statuette of Kurokawa herself.

"What do you think? Beautiful, isn't she? I had them go back sixteen times to get the teeth just right."

"We don't care! Just get to the point already!!"

"Well, somebody woke up on the wrong side of the forest, my dear Panda. You realize this game requires patience, don't you? In the original, you take these swords and slide them into the barrel, and if the pirate pops up, you lose. However, this version is different. In this game, when the tyrant pops out, you win."

"…Hmm? Then we just gotta keep jammin' swords in until it does! C'mon, Milo!"

"H-hey, let me finish—!"

But Bisco immediately picked up one of the swords on the table and pushed it into a random slot. When he did, he heard a crackle, and Shishi recoiled in pain.

"Gah!!"

"…Shishi?!"

"That's why you've got to let me finish, silly. You see, if you put a sword in the wrong slot, then the queen there gets a little shock. The level increases with each failed attempt. That was level one, and just for reference, level four can fry a person's brain in five seconds."

"Th-that's horrible!"

Milo shuddered as Shishi groaned and spasmed.

"This isn't a puzzle; it's just random!! You want us to bet Shishi's life on a game of chance?!"

"Well, they can't all be riddles, Nekoyanagi. Sometimes you just need a little dumb luck. Like, do you cut the red wire or the blue one?"

Suddenly, Shishi called out. "B-Brother! Milo…! I…I have already died twice. There is no worth in saving me now! I could ask for no greater honor than to be killed by Brother's hand! Do it! Please…"

"Oh, you're going to make me cry. But you just don't get it, do you? Pleading for death is only going to stay Akaboshi's hand!!"

"Okay."

"...Whaaat?!"

Bisco met Shishi's gaze and nodded once. Then he immediately picked up the next sword, jamming it into another slot as the shock helmet crackled once more.

"Bisco!! Stop it! There must be another way!"

"Yes, have you gone insane, Akaboshi? Your student's life is on the line here! Can't we at least have a few seconds of inner conflict?!"

"The longer we draw it out, the worse it's gonna be. Here goes another."

Bisco could not be stopped. He picked up a third sword, and a fourth. Each time he fitted them in the slots, a jolt of electricity ran through Shishi and caused her pale body to contort in pain.

"Bisco, please!!"

His heart about to burst, Milo looked imploringly at his partner. For all Bisco's conviction, he was sweating even more heavily than usual, and his face screwed up in regret whenever the Benibishi girl screamed. Even after Bisco placed the sixth sword, there were still over thirty slots remaining.

"Next is level seven! A shock powerful enough to take out a king turtle! Our little prisoner will be scorched black in an instant, so think long and hard about where you're going to put this one, Akaboshi!"

"Brother!! Finish me off! Do it now!!"

Shishi was screaming through the glass. Bisco wasted no time picking up a red-colored sword and slamming it into his chosen slot.

"Oh dear, now look at what you've gone and done! That's the end of the—"

Pwoof!

Before Kurokawa could finish, the barrel activated, launching the pop-up tyrant into the air.

"Whaaat?!"

The figure was flung with such force that it rocketed straight up and cracked the ceiling, lodging itself there. Bisco and Milo could only stare at its bottom half in shock as bits of ceiling plaster fell to the floor.

"I-impossible! You guessed right?!"

There was a loud *Pshoo...* as the electricity flowing from Shishi's mask was cut off, and the girl fell limp with exhaustion. Milo ran up as close as he could and, after looking her over for a moment, turned to Bisco and nodded.

"It's a good thing you were quick to decide, Bisco. Looks like she's still alive!"

For a while, no sound came from the speakers. Then...

"...I see... Not quite the scene I had in mind, but by overcoming your doubt, you were able to minimize the time the girl spent exposed to the shocks. Simple in theory, but hard to pull off. I think we're starting to see what makes you such a compelling hero, Akaboshi."

"Shut up, Kurokawa! Get rid of this glass so I can treat her!!"

"Oh, don't worry—we'll take care of that. I'm more concerned about where to go from here. You see, it was certainly a dramatic scene, but it was over so fast I'm not sure how we'll pad out the run time. I suppose we'll have to bring back one of our scrapped ideas. Bear with me a moment..."

At this, the speaker cut out and all was silent. On the other side of the glass, the Immie from earlier reappeared and gave a short bow. He then lifted the unconscious Shishi up over his shoulder and disappeared into the wings.

Milo watched him go with a scowl, then remembered himself and turned back to Bisco. By the time he was once again at his partner's side, Bisco's tension seemed to have dissipated entirely, and he was back to his usual sour look.

"That was amazing, Bisco!" he said. "You were so brave! I could never have done what you did..."

"Brave? Nah, I wasn't brave. I just knew it would grow after the seventh."

"Grow? What would?"

"A little bit of my blood. I put it on the tip of the first sword."

Bisco showed Milo his thumb, where there was a small bloody mark. In its partially awakened state, Bisco's blood gave off a sunny, golden glow.

"I did it while that asshole was distracted readin' out the rules," he continued. "Then all I had to do was slam the swords in hard enough that it'd grow."

"Th-then…you never picked the right slot at all!!"

"Nah, it was the Rust-Eater that pushed the figure out. Weak enough that it wouldn't look too suspicious. The hard part was doin' it before Shishi kicked the bucket. I knew she had it in her, though."

Milo just stared, dumbfounded.

B-Bisco's really smart, in his own way!

Bisco had played the image everyone had of him to his own advantage. He'd acted out the role of the hasty, short-tempered fool, all the while executing his plan right under Kurokawa's nose. It wasn't the first time Bisco had used the spores to his advantage, of course. But this time he'd come up with a way to subvert the rules mere moments after being suddenly thrust into a new and confusing situation. Milo had to admit, his partner was a lot cleverer than people gave him credit for.

"…I just thought about what Jabi would do," said Bisco, folding his arms. "I've lived through ten years of that man's schemes. I'll never measure up to him, though. He always said I didn't have a head for strategy."

"But you managed to outwit Kurokawa!" Milo retorted. "That's got to count for something! You've changed, Bisco, and I bet Jabi would be proud if he could see you now!"

"…Proud? Of me?"

"Yeah! Of course!"

Bisco looked up at the ceiling, wondering what to make of Milo's claim. But instead of an answer, he just blushed. Seeing that, Milo couldn't control himself and bounded over to his partner's side, taking his hands and shaking them up and down in glee. Bisco cried out in surprise and shook him off, placing his finger to his lips and going, "Shhh! Be quiet, or Kurokawa's gonna know we were cheating! Remember, she's still got Shishi and Pawoo under her thumb!"

"I'm not sure Kurokawa would even care," Milo replied with a shrug.

"Akaboshi! Nekoyanagi! Sorry for the wait! The next room's ready for you, so come on through!"

At the sudden return of Kurokawa's voice, the two boys stood up straight and cleared their throats.

"Now, just wait right there, and I'll send someone to fetch you. Oh, and feel free to take the Kurokawa figure if you like. A little memento of this adven—"

Ker-rash!

All of a sudden, the whole room shook as if they were in an earthquake. The two boys shared a confused glance as panicked voices came over the speaker.

"Wh-what?! What was that?!"

"Director! Director! It's the prisoner! He's woken up! He's still hazy, but we can't contain him!"

"He's woken up, you say?" There was irritation and annoyance in Kurokawa's voice. *"Don't be silly. We pumped him with enough tranquilizers to take down* ten *king turtles! He should be fast asleep until we give him the antidote!"*

Crash! Crash!

"NRRRRGHHH!"

Along with the noise, the two boys heard a familiar cry—like the king of the dead rising out of hell itself.

"Bisco, that voice!" cried Milo as he tried to peek into the next room.

"…!! Milo, look out!" yelled Bisco. He leaped over, grabbed his partner, and jumped back. Only a moment later, a blast demolished the wall, and a giant of a man appeared in the breach, clad head to toe in navy-blue armor, and with hot steam rising off his body.

"What is the meaning of this…?" he muttered.

"Y-Your Honor!!"

Of course, this giant was none other than the Lord High Overseer,

Someyoshi Satahabaki, a man whose name was known and feared by criminals across the land.

"For what reason…do you imprison me without CAAAUSE?!!!"

Satahabaki brought his wrists, bound together in thick steel manacles, in front of his face. He clenched his bare teeth, like white pillars, and pulled. The muscles all over his body tensed, and soon the metal cuffs began to crack and break apart.

"I shall not…tolerate…this injustice…"

"He's breaking out on his own? That's ridiculous! Forget it; we've seen enough. Everyone evacuate! Protect the equipment!"

"How dare…you imprison…the Lord High OVERSEERRR!"

Clang!

The manacles snapped in two, and Satahabaki slammed his freed fists into the ground. The impact shook loose several lights from above, and the weakly constructed set began to collapse.

"Wh-whoa there, big guy! You didn't have to wreck the place!"

"The tranquilizer hasn't worn off yet! He's still woozy, and he's letting his anger take over! We've got to get out of here before the whole place collapses on us!"

"KAHHH!"

Satahabaki thrust his huge arms, like tree trunks, into the floor. They began to throb, and all across Kurokawa's Professional Psycho Thriller House, the walls began to bulge, until *Bwoom! Bwoom!* Cherry blossom trees burst through, breaking down the supports.

"Waaagh?!"

Tossed to and fro by the sprouting cherry trees, the boys finally tumbled through a broken bit of wall, narrowly escaping with their lives. Bisco picked Milo up off the floor, and the two of them dashed away just as one final tree burst from the building, shooting them up toward Powder Mountain's peak.

"Th-that was close…!" Bisco sighed as the two of them sat down, exhausted. Above them, the fleeing form of Kurokawa's craft streaked across the sky.

"Wh-what a force of nature! Aah, look at the set! He's ruined it! Whose idea was it to cast that big lug?!"

"Wasn't it yours, Director?"

"Whatever. We'll have to cut that last scene, but otherwise we have enough to work with. Akaboshi! I've left a message with that Benibishi girl! Speak with her to find out where you're going next!"

Bisco and Milo watched in shock as the Dacarabia disappeared over the horizon. Meanwhile, pink cherry blossoms fell like snow, collecting in their hair.

"Look this way, please, Shishi. Now, open wide and say 'Aah.'"

"A-aaahhh."

"You'll feel a small jab at the base of your tongue… Okay, all done!"

Shishi grimaced as a bitter sensation spread throughout her mouth. After Milo's treatment was done, the Benibishi children rescued during the first demo round came running over to her.

"King Shishi! Dr. Panda, is King Shishi going to die?"

"She's fine!" said Milo. "Shishi's very strong, you know. That's how she was able to save you all from the cherry trees."

"Please, Milo. I just did what any king would for their people."

"King Shishi, your breath smells weird. Like burned Kaso cakes."

"Ha, now you've done it. Come here, you little troublemakers!" said Shishi, capturing the children and exhaling into their faces.

"Waah!"

Milo breathed a sigh of relief at their frolicking.

"I'm just glad to see there aren't any lingering effects," he said. "You may be strong, but you're still just a girl— Er, I mean…"

Seeing Milo fumble his words, Shishi held back a chuckle.

"It's okay, Milo. You're a doctor, and biologically, I am a girl. I understand. It's just…perhaps Mepaosha was right about me. I was a fool. A fool who let her people be captured."

"…"

"If Father were here, instead of me, then maybe this never would have happened. Perhaps I'm just..."

"Stop it, Shishi. Don't say any more."

Milo crouched down beside her and lifted her head. She gazed into his starlight eyes, her lip quivering.

"Do you think Housen was always King Housen?" he asked.

"...Milo? What do you mean...?"

"Your father had to go through all the same things to get there. Screwing up, crawling through the mud... I'm sure he had thoughts just like yours, both good and bad. It's not fair to compare your darkest moments to his brightest, is it?"

Even Shishi couldn't hide from Milo's sparkling gaze. She silently nodded.

"But Housen knew he had gone too far. That's why he staged his final gambit in an effort to purify the Benibishi."

"His final gambit?"

"For you..."

""...to kill him.""

Shishi completed the thought alongside Milo. Then she silently wrapped her arms around herself.

She thought back to that decisive blow. All she had felt as her blade sliced the king's flesh was his love and acceptance. It was a pain nobody else knew, and one she'd tried hard to paint over in blood.

"The only one who hasn't forgiven you, Shishi, is you."

"..."

"Ever since you took the crown, the Benibishi have been gaining more and more of their individuality. You've been following in your father's footsteps, but you've also begun to open a path of your own. What would he think if you threw all that away?"

Shishi was silent for a moment, then she breathed deeply and let out a bitter laugh.

"I should have you beheaded, you know. That's no way to speak to a king."

"Huh?! Th-that's a joke, right?!"

"Ha-ha-ha! You're brave, Milo. Not as brave as Brother, of course. I should take a page from his book. He's never content to walk in another's shadow."

"Hmm? I wouldn't be so sure about that..."

Milo smiled and cast his eyes over to where Bisco was standing. Then he whispered:

"He's quite devoted, too, you know. To his own father."

Bisco, meanwhile, was engaged in a conversation of his own with Satahabaki.

"Gaze upon these marvelous blossoms, Akaboshi! Despite months of lying idle, it is good to see my Bountiful Art has not yet waned!"

Bisco, however, was in no mood for flower-gazing.

"It's your brain I'm worried about!" he roared. "You damn near took us out with those blossoms, and Shishi and the kids as well!"

"Nearly, but I did not. Now, was my prudence the cause, or your heaven-sent luck? That is the question... Aah, 'tis cleeear a sign of for-tuuune to round out the spriiing!"

"It's the middle of freakin' fall!"

Satahabaki raised his scepter to the strum of a *shamisen* as blossoms fell gently around him. Bisco just watched, his face twitching. The judge had a real habit of running away with the conversation—it was no wonder Kurokawa got sick of him so quickly.

Luckily, Shishi picked just then to walk over, and Bisco scurried behind her. "Someyoshi," she said. "These are splendid blossoms indeed, but I fear we must be on our way. Tell me, were you ignorant of Mepaosha's secrets this entire time?"

"That has been weighing heavily on my mind," Satahabaki replied. "As I recall, she came highly recommended by Matoba Heavy Industries. I made her and Gopis my vice-wardens in order to monitor my dictatorship. She was skilled at her tasks, and I never thought her any more ambitious than her counterpart. I was blind..."

Monitor...??

So you admit it was a dictatorship, Your Honor?

"Regardless, to oppose her now, with the power of the camellia at her back, would be suicide for all the Benibishi. Akaboshi, you must do something!"

"All right, all right! Milo's workin' on it!"

Bisco looked to his partner, who nodded and turned to Shishi.

"That's right. I'm working on a vaccine that will counteract the power of the Rust flower. It should be able to undo Pawoo's brainwashing and that of everyone else affected."

"If you say so, Milo, then it must be true. Tell us, is there anything we can do to help?"

Milo thought for a moment before answering.

"...Actually, there is. I need a sample of the Benibishi's Florescence to complete the vaccine. Is there any way you could give me one?"

Milo looked at her sheepishly. Perhaps it was a terrible thing to ask, given the girl's traumatic past with her flower, but Shishi gave a firm nod.

"A trifling request, Milo. Take anything you want. In fact, take this..."

Shishi closed her eyes and focused, and her wrist glowed gold. Ivy sprouted forth, taking shape. When Milo recognized its form, he blurted out a name.

"Th-the Lion's Crimson Sword?!"

Shishi winced as she tore the ivy sword from her arm, then smiled and handed it over to Milo.

"As much as I would love to join you, I fear I can only do so in spirit. I am not yet strong enough to protect my people and also offer my aid. Please take this, so that at least part of me may help you on your journey."

"Thank you so much, Shishi!"

"Only two people have ever bested me at the sword," she said, stroking Milo's sky-blue hair. "Father...and you." Her voice was tinged with love and affection, but also with a little regret. "Allow me to protect my brother, Milo. Allow me to stand by his side."

Milo gazed into her earnest eyes and nodded. Bisco, standing a little ways off, looked at the pair and said, "That's not fair. How come Milo gets a new toy, and I don't?"

"I understand your plight, Akaboshi. Here, pray take my scepter with you."

"...Wh-whoa!! How the hell am I supposed to lug this thing around, you colossal dumbass?!"

"Come, Someyoshi," said Shishi, stepping in to rescue Bisco from an impromptu slapstick act. "Parting is such sweet sorrow, but we must not stop them. They must hurry to their next destination, lest yet more innocent lives be lost."

Bisco and Milo stiffened, listening attentively for Shishi's next words.

"Mepaosha has told me where you must go," she continued. "The next location is..."

✳ ✳ ✳

"Banryouji Temple?" asked Pawoo.

"Yep."

"The head temple, in northern Iwate Prefecture? *That* Banryouji?"

"That's what I said."

Kurokawa was busy looking over the recorded footage, occasionally exclaiming things like, "And then...*bam!*" or "That's it, Akaboshi, you sexy man!" Whenever fresh inspiration came to mind, she would pull out a red pen and scribble into the script.

"We need a scene with all the women Akaboshi's helped along the way," Kurokawa went on. "Otherwise, the second act is going to drag on. I asked the queen to pass on my message, so Akaboshi should be here shortly."

"But, Director, unlike the other locations, Banryouji is outside of Imihama's control. The people call it the last bastion of religion in Japan."

"Uh-huh."

"Of all its leaders, Banryouji's High Priest Ochagama is perhaps the most skilled in the mystic arts. *And* he has the backing of the other sects, such as the Kusabira sect of—"

"Oh, shut up, shut up, shut up! *You're* supposed to deal with that stuff! You took out Actagawa and those Benibishi, didn't you?! What's a few out-of-touch Buddhists to a woman with the Rust flower on her side?"

"...Understood."

Pawoo's expression was unreadable behind the shadow of her skull-cap. Kurokawa paid the woman no heed. It seemed she had complete faith in the strength of her brainwashing.

"However!" Kurokawa declared. "I have a request for you this time. They say the priestesses of the Kusabira sect are all pretty ladies. Capture a few of them alive for me, would you? We can use them as extras."

"Alive? But, Director, those priestesses are extremely powerful..."

"I thought you were an expert in nonlethal takedowns? Surely you can handle it," Kurokawa replied. Then she began humming to herself. "We'll need them alive for the big romance scene. I want to treat Akaboshi after all he's done for this production. We'll set up a hidden camera and—"

"Romance...scene?"

"Oh, um..."

Kurokawa fell silent as Pawoo's voice took on a dark tone. Her emotions, usually silenced by the brainwashing, were beginning to boil.

"And who, pray tell, is participating in this scene?" she spat.

"Wait, wait!! Did I say Akaboshi? I meant...er...a pair of star-crossed lovers reunited by the gruff, loner protagonist! You know, like in *Yojimbo!*"

Somehow, Pawoo seemed convinced by this patchy explanation. She returned to her usual, brainwashed monotone.

"...Director. We will soon be arriving at Banryouji."

"G-great, great! I...just need to dash to the little girls' room."

Kurokawa excused herself and ran to the onboard bathrooms, wiping her sweat in the mirror.

That woman is triggered by the strangest things. My brainwashing is solid, but I get the feeling all it'll take is one slipup and she'll be at my throat. I'd better not let her see the—

"...Oh, shit, the script!"

Kurokawa hurried back, but Pawoo and the Immie guards were nowhere to be seen. It appeared they'd already commenced the mission. And there, on Kurokawa's desk, was the script.

"Oh... Oh no..."

It looked as if it had been crushed in the iron grip of a monster before being discarded. The title at the top of the page read *"Akaboshi Harem Scene."*

＊ ＊ ＊

Banryouji Temple was positioned atop an enormous boulder in the Iwate wastes. One long, winding path snaked around the boulder to its peak, and the way was lined with scriptures carved into the rock face, so that travelers could deepen their understanding on their way to the summit.

Upon reaching the end of this path, pilgrims had to scale the famous "Hundred and Eight Steps" before arriving at the temple proper. These steps were each about one-and-a-half meters tall, and their existence was said to be the primary reason that modern believers were all so rugged and tough. "No salvation without exertion" was the mantra of the day.

It was in complete defiance of this long and pious tradition with which, like a shooting star across the night sky, Bisco and Milo catapulted through the air on their jet-powered crab to land directly and conveniently on the hundred-and-seventh step.

Ker-rash!!

The two boys leaped out of the smoking crater and rolled along the ground. Milo stood and looked back at Actagawa, letting out a yelp of surprise as he saw the steam rising off the crab's body.

"Actagawa?! ...Oh, phew, he's just gone to sleep."

Bisco, meanwhile, gazed up at the majesty of the temple, before suddenly grabbing Milo and shaking him by the collar.

"The hell do you think you're doin'?! You tryin' to get us both cursed?! We're supposed to climb these stairs, not just drop outta the sky! These Banryouji gods watch over us Mushroom Keepers! What are we gonna do if you piss 'em off?!"

"Oh, calm down! Don't you think some things are more important than that?!"

Milo gripped Bisco's nose with surprising strength, as if training an unruly hound, and twisted. Bisco cried out in pain, rubbing his bright-red nose with tears in his eyes, but Milo only shushed him.

"I made Actagawa go as fast as I could, but I wasn't able to catch up to Kurokawa," he said. "Anything could be waiting for us inside there, so keep your guard up!"

"…All right. Let's split up and head inside," said Bisco. He was still rubbing his nose, but his expression was serious. "Kurokawa's got all her attention on me. If we go different ways, she can't capture both of us. Whatever happens, one of us can still save the other."

"Okay! So who's taking the front?"

"Me, obviously. You go around back."

"Knew you'd say that. Don't overdo it, Bisco!"

Without waiting for Bisco to finish, Milo turned and was already on his way to the back of the temple. Bisco watched him leave but stopped before heading in himself.

Come to think of it, this is my first time here. I'd better apologize for breakin' the rules.

Putting away his bow, Bisco lowered his head before the main gates, then tossed a few coins in the offering box nearby.

"We Mushroom Keepers share your beliefs through the guidance of Enbiten, Yoten, Keppaten, and Josanten. In the spirit of goodwill between our people, I humbly ask that you forgive our trespasses…"

"Whatever are you muttering about over there?"

"…Huh?!"

Bisco opened his eyes to find a familiar face standing in front of the main doors.

"...I-it's you!"

Fluffy white hair and a dainty figure. Her left eye held open in a permanent, unblinking gaze. The person before him was none other than the high priestess of the Kusabira sect, a girl so famous and revered throughout the land that anyone would have recognized her.

"Amli!" he cried in surprise. "The hell are you doin' here?"

"I could ask you the same thing," she replied. Peering curiously at Bisco's face, she smiled. "I never thought the fearless Mushroom Keepers would have cause to entreat their gods for anything."

"'Course we do. Without the gods' help, our arrows wouldn't strike true."

"An admirable creed, Mr. Bisco, sir, but I fear your humility might cause some distress. You see, here in the Kusabira sect, we worship *you* as our god, and a god can't exactly pray to other gods, can he?"

Bisco suddenly felt as though something was off. It wasn't like Amli to act this subdued when the two hadn't seen each other for so long.

"Now, take off your shoes so we can show you around. Please step inside."

"Show me around? This ain't even your temple!"

"Come, my fellow priestesses. Our god has returned. Show him to the inner sanctum."

"Listen to me! Where's Tirol's old man? Where's—? Whoa!"

Suddenly, two robed priestesses appeared out of nowhere and hooked Bisco's arms. With beautiful smiles, they hoisted him up and carried him away.

"W-wait! What's goin' on?!"

"Worried about High Priest Ochagama? Why, you really have changed, Mr. Bisco, sir," said Amli with a chuckle. "You're a shining example to all of us mere mortals."

"L-let go! Let go, I said! Amli, tell 'em!"

"However, it must be terribly stressful putting on a good face all the time. Allow us to provide you with some comfort..."

As the two priestesses dragged Bisco along, Amli danced and twirled ahead of him.

"Just think of this all as a dream, Mr. Bisco, sir. It shall be a wonderful, most pleasurable dream—I can promise you that."

"Come now, Akaboshi. If you struggle, I won't be able to focus."

"Focus on what?! Get off me! I'm here to rescue you!!"

"There's nothing to fear. Once you've had a taste of my massage, you won't desire anything else… I've always wanted to test my art on a divine canvas."

"That's not fair, Mother! I had him first! I want Mr. Bisco to see *my* arts!"

"I'm afraid this isn't the same as your children's games, Amli."

"Grrr!!"

"Both of you, shaddup! Get the hell off me!"

They were in a room that looked suspiciously like a bedchamber, deep within the temple. As a result of his careless struggles, Bisco had inhaled a considerable amount of the dense incense filling the space. It wasn't poisoned, or else he would have been quicker to react, but it seemed to contain some kind of medicinal compound that made his eyelids feel weighty.

Upon entering the bedchamber, a half-naked Raskeni had pinned Bisco to the bed with her formidable strength. Even if he could escape her grip, her loyal warrior priestesses would ensure that he didn't leave the room.

S-somethin' ain't right! Even for a joke, this has gone way too far!

"What powerful muscles," Raskeni mused. "Like a wild beast. And your eyes, those of a hunter. They send a chill down my spine. Oh, what was wrong with me? Why did I ever serve that awful man, when I could have had a boy like you…?"

With the lightest, most tantalizing touch, Raskeni traced her long fingernails down Bisco's neck. He was overcome with a sensation of pure, utter fear unlike anything he'd felt before.

"Waaaagh!!"

"E-erm, Mother? Don't you think you're getting a little—?"

"Silence, child!"

Raskeni was not her usual calm self. Right now, she was like a starving wolf eyeing her prey.

"You're the one who's not playing fair!" she roared. "You get to cavort around with Akaboshi and Nekoyanagi all you like, and nobody says anything because you're just a child! Why, if I didn't have to be your mother, I'd be out there, too!!"

"Wh-whatever is the cause of all this harsh language, Mother?!"

"Come, Akaboshi. Let me help you fill your lungs. This is part of the process. It's most certainly not because I want to kiss you."

"K-kiss me…?! S-stop it! Hey!"

"Now relax…"

His head and shoulders pinned in place, all Bisco could do was look up at Raskeni's inverted smile. As she slowly brought her face closer to his, Bisco's face contorted in fear. He was more terrified than he'd ever been in his life. Pushing his voice to the limits, he cried out.

"MILOOOO! HELP MEEEEE!!"

Ker-rash!

A black meteor came crashing through the ceiling and landed in the center of the room. The cold autumn air rushed in, dispelling the incense and putting an end to the steamy atmosphere that had built up inside.

"Tch! Who dares interfere?"

Raskeni leaped back and summoned a spear of Rust in her hand.

"Reveal yourself! We are administering to a god! This is an act of blasphemy!"

"Blasphemy…?" the intruder spat back in a menacing tone. "You dare speak of blasphemy…?"

A splinter of wood cracked beneath the figure's boots as they stepped into the light. *Fwoom, fwoom, fwoom!* The weapon in their fingers twirled, cutting through the air. It was a hexagonal rod of steel weighing twelve kilos.

"You're the one laying your hands on another woman's husband!"

screamed Pawoo. Her spirit seemed to ignite the very air around her, blasting away the rubble on the ground.

"Aaagh!" "Eek!"

Raskeni and Amli tumbled off Bisco as Pawoo swung her staff, striking the ground between them. A rush of air destroyed the bedroom floor and nearly tore their thin clothes to shreds.

"Oh, Pawoo! Thank the gods!"

Bisco found his mind steadily returning as he lay in Pawoo's arms, gazing beneath her visor into her eyes.

"You saved me! ...Wait, aren't you still brainwashed?"

"Was it good?"

"H-huh?"

"That kiss. Was it better than mine?"

What the hell's wrong with her?!

Bisco hadn't the faintest idea what Pawoo was trying to ascertain, but he got the sense that the wrong answer might spell his doom, and so, mind racing, he chose to shake his head as fast as he could.

"..."

"..."

"...Of course not. I just thought I'd ask."

Her eyes were darkened from the brainwashing, but for just one brief second, Bisco saw a glimmer of satisfaction pass through them. At that, he inferred he must have given the correct answer.

"We'll talk later," she said. "For now, I must deal with these women..."

"Y-yeah! They've all been brainwashed! Do you know how to—?"

"...by killing them."

"Wh-what?"

"Hi-yah!!"

The black whirlwind tore through the room, sending the priestesses flying with nothing more than the force emanating from her staff. Shrieks were heard as they went sailing into the walls, knocking them down and revealing the hidden cameras set up on the other side.

"Y-you were filming this?!"

"Fret not, my love. I shall destroy the evidence...after I deal with these harlots. Especially you, Raskeni!! I'll turn you into mincemeat!"

"S-stop it!" cried Bisco. "Don't kill her!"

"Yes, stand down, Captain! Thanks to you, this entire scene has been ruined. You're just the assistant director, remember?! Meddling with the set is above your authority!!"

Kurokawa's voice came from high up in the air. As soon as she heard it, Pawoo froze and brought her staff back to her side.

"Oh, and it was all going so well, too. The look on Akaboshi's face right at the end... Well, we'll fix it in post. We just reached the end of the reel anyway."

"Kurokawa! It ain't fair to harm the hostages! Bring Amli and the others back to normal now!"

"Oh, don't worry," said Kurokawa dismissively. *"I didn't use the Rust flower on them. It would've dulled their senses, and I wanted this to be sexy. This is just an ordinary stupefying drug. Your panda friend should be more than capable of countering its effects."*

She sighed. *"This scene's a bust. We'll head back to the studio for now. I'll let you know the schedule in good time, Akaboshi, so just sit tight. Assistant! Get back here! We're leaving!"*

Pawoo turned, ready to jump into the air and rejoin her master, when Bisco grabbed her hand.

"Pawoo!"

"Release me. I have a job to complete."

"I'm sorry for gettin' you wrapped up in all this," he said. "Don't worry. I'll find a way to free you. Just wait."

"..."

Their eyes, jade and indigo, locked in a magnetic pull. It was Pawoo who broke away first, shaking off Bisco's hand and leaping out through the broken roof to catch hold of a ladder dangling from the Dacarabia.

Bisco watched her go, then cast a glance around the pulverized remains of the bedchamber.

"A-Akaboshi...help me...," said Raskeni.

"I—I think all my bones are broken!" Amli cried.

"*Now* you want my help? And after the shit you two pulled...," he muttered, cracking his neck and lumbering over to pull the pair free from the rubble.

☰ ⚻ ⵔ Ꮎ⚻ **9**

"...No, it's still not pure enough. Come on, Amli, focus!"

"Are we not done yet, Mr. Milo, sir? I fear if you take any more, I shall wither up like a dead plant!"

"And you'd deserve it, after what you did to Bisco. Now, come on. I need to finish this medicine!"

"I—I told you, that was Kurokawa's doing! I had no agency in the matt— Eep! Don't be so rough!"

Milo held Amli's head so that she couldn't run. His mantra cube spun rapidly above her vacant eye socket, drawing forth the Rust power that dwelled inside the high priestess's body. A raging torrent of purple-glowing rust streamed out of her head and into the cube.

"Yes, looking good. Just a little more, Amli!"

"Make it stoppp!!"

As Milo's emerald cube absorbed more and more of Amli's power, it turned a deeper and deeper shade of violet. At last, after absorbing everything it could, it had become a shimmering black.

"Yes! All done!"

"Fwehhh..."

Amli promptly conked out, and Milo dashed in to catch her. After lowering her gently to the floor, he turned his eyes on the jet-black cube in his hand and gulped.

Before him on the table stood his medicine mixer. Each of its cylindrical tanks made an impressive whirring sound as Milo's special mixing liquid bubbled inside them.

Suspended in the liquid of the first two were Chaika's Ghost Hail crystal and a flower from the Lion's Crimson Sword.

"This is the final ingredient…!!"

Milo sent his Rust-saturated cube into the third cylinder. As he did, all three liquids shone brightly, and the mixing machine began to rattle.

"Uh-oh!"

Milo immediately pulled the drive lever, engaging the motor. The three cylinders gave off a dazzling light, and then…

Bang!

"What the—?! Milo!!"

Bisco, who had been sleeping, shot up off the floor. All he could see where Milo had been sitting was a cloud of black smoke.

"Milo, what happened?! We bein' attacked? Dammit!!"

Bisco drew his knife and was just about to plunge into the cloud when Milo came staggering out of it.

"M-Milo?"

"It's done," Milo said, before coughing up smoke. His skin was all sooty and black, and his sky-blue hair was frizzy and scorched.

"Done? What's done?!"

"One sec."

Carrying Amli under his arm, Milo walked over and laid her on the ground. Then he rummaged around in his pocket, pulling out a syringe filled with an unknown silvery substance.

"Wh-what's that??" asked Bisco.

The silver spores within it danced like bubbles rushing up through boiling water. Even Bisco could tell it was a very powerful serum.

"They may look like ordinary Ghost Hail spores," Milo explained, "but they've been combined with antibiotics made from the Florescence and the Rust. We can use this to counteract Kurokawa's Rust flower."

"You made the vaccine already?! That was fast!!"

"I already knew how to beat Kurokawa," said Milo. "I just needed the ingredients: highly concentrated mushrooms, flowers, and Rust."

Puffs of black smoke streamed from Milo's mouth as he spoke, and he glanced at the syringe again. Its silvery glow lit up his face.

"If we can inject this into the Rust flower, we win! Let's apply it to your arrows and save Pawoo!"

"But the flower grows at the back of the neck. How am I supposed to get to it?"

"Well, you could…er…"

"Never mind. I'll think of somethin'."

Bisco took a corner of his cloak and wiped the soot from his partner's panda face.

"Mmrgh."

"You've swapped colors… Hold still. I'm tryin' to clean it off."

"Hey, Bisco?"

"We can't dance to Kurokawa's tune anymore. It's time to take the fight to her."

"Who do you like more, Pawoo or Raskeni?"

"Tomorrow, we head for Imihama. Get some sleep."

"So you can't answer? Is that because you feel guilty? Shame on you, Bisco. As Pawoo's brother, I'm disappointed."

"The hell have I done to deserve this?! What is it with you two?!"

As the boys descended into another one of their pointless quarrels, Actagawa sat atop the temple roof, as noble and majestic as though he had been carved from brass. The moon glinted off his carapace as the giant crab looked out over the wasteland like a guardian spirit.

✳ ✳ ✳

"Good luck, Mr. Bisco!!"

"Akaboshi! You let that Kurokawa beat you, and I'll come down to hell myself and kill you again!"

In the glimmering sunlight, the Calvero Shellsand Sea flickered in all the colors of the rainbow. Nuts, Kousuke, and the other children cheered and cried out in support as Actagawa circled Tetsujin Town one last time before departing southward.

"So those kids managed to get out of Imihama?" asked Bisco.

"It was Pawoo. She was able to buy time for them to escape... I'm glad they're doing okay."

Milo was looking over his shoulder and waving back at the town when his eyes fell on Plum. She seemed to have grown quite a bit since their last meeting, and as soon as the two made eye contact, Plum blushed and turned away without saying anything.

"Remember all the shit we went through last time we were here?" remarked Bisco. "Feels like cheatin' to just fly over it all."

"Aren't you warming up to it? The travel is smooth, and you have to admit it's kind of cool. A rocket-powered crab!"

"Bullshit. Soon as we beat Kurokawa, I'm takin' these things off!"

Though he wasn't fully sold, Bisco was starting to see the genius of old Japanese technology. What had once been a three-day journey now only took the boys a few hours, and already they had passed beyond the sea's edge.

The driftweeds below were starting to shed balls of algae, the color of autumn leaves, that would carry their seeds on the wind across the plains.

"We're over the Driftweed Plains now," Bisco pointed out. "We're close enough to Imihama that Kurokawa might see us, so watch out."

"Roger!" came Milo's enthusiastic reply. Then, all of a sudden, his face froze. "Bisco, what's that?!"

"Hmm?"

With a *Boom, Boom*, two objects appeared out of nowhere in the air directly ahead of them, softly drifting like a pair of parachutes. They were round, with silvery skin that occasionally crackled with lightning.

"Are those...mushrooms?" Milo asked.

When Bisco saw them, his eyes went wide. "...Electroshrooms!!" he exclaimed, drawing his bow and loosing a pair of arrows. The projectiles struck the electroshrooms before they'd fully charged, bursting them like balloons and sending them falling to earth.

"Milo! We have to turn back. Somethin's not right!"

"What is it?"

"Electroshrooms are a Mushroom Keeper crab huntin' trick! It's not Kurokawa! I didn't think it was possible, but we're probably facin'...!!"

Before Bisco could find the words to express himself, their foe struck again. Several arrows came flying up from ground level. The electroshroom spores still hung in the air, and when the arrows hit them, they exploded into a line of mushrooms that blocked Actagawa's path.

"Waagh! Actagawa, swerve, swerve!!"

Boom! Boom! Boom!

Whoever the enemy was, they had laid this trap ahead of time. The air was already thick with spores, and when the arrows triggered them, the resulting electroshrooms caged Actagawa in, cutting off all escape. The shock passed straight through the steelcrab's carapace, numbing his limbs and causing him to lose control of his thrusters.

"Actagawa's goin' down!" shouted Bisco. "Milo, hen-of-the-woods, on my mark!"

"Got it!"

Actagawa fell out of the sky, taking several of the electroshrooms with him. Bisco and Milo aimed their bows at the ground.

Pchew! Gaboom!

Mushrooms bloomed with explosive force, saving the trio from a crash landing but throwing the two riders clear into a conveniently placed driftweed.

"Owww... Who would do something like that?"

"Milo! Get up! They're coming!"

As if to emphasize the point, an arrow whizzed by and landed with a *Thunk!* in the ground between the two boys. It immediately exploded into a cluster of bright-yellow oyster mushrooms, flinging the pair apart.

Milo righted himself in the air and gazed in shock at the result of the attack.

"Mushrooms?! B-but that means...!"

"Oyster mushrooms are the art of my clan," said Bisco. Milo had never seen him look so grim. "That's who we're up against… The Shikoku Mushroom Keepers!"

"*Excellent deduction, Akaboshi! Aaah-ha-ha-ha!*" Kurokawa's mad laughter echoed across the Driftweed Plains. "*Do you have any idea how hard it is to brainwash fifty Mushroom Keepers? But the show must go on!*"

"Kurokawa!! Where are you? Show yourself!!"

"*The genius Dr. Panda has gone to all three locations and succeeded in obtaining the ingredients he needs to complete the Rust flower vaccine!*"

Huh?!

"*However, he only has enough for three doses. Isn't that right?*"

D-dammit! She knew I'd been working on the vaccine this entire time!

Kurokawa chuckled, amused beyond belief at the accuracy of her prediction.

"*It's time to see our protagonist's inner conflict. Will Akaboshi do what is necessary to succeed? Will you slaughter scores of your former comrades just to save one woman? Cut them down mercilessly for your one true love? Well, Akaboshi?!*"

"Shut the hell up!!"

"Bisco, watch out!!"

A Mushroom Keeper emerged from his hiding place, and Milo leaped for his partner. He managed to tackle Bisco out of the path of the arrow, but it created a yellow oyster mushroom that blasted them both to the ground. Just then, another arrow landed beside them, and a cluster of mushrooms threw them high up into the air. Meanwhile, more and more Mushroom Keepers came out from behind driftweeds, firing arrow after arrow at the boys. If just one of them landed a hit, the pair would be torn to shreds.

Milo landed atop an ancient, rusted tank, destroying the gun turret and crushing the frame. Bisco grabbed his stunned partner and pulled him free just seconds before a hail of mushroom arrows blew the tank apart.

"*Cough! Cough!*"

"Milo! Keep it together!"

"We have to run, Bisco!" cried Milo as he popped his dislocated shoulder back into place. "You can't bloody your hands here; it's what Kurokawa wants! I won't let her boss you around anymore!"

"I know! But...!!"

Modern Japan was home to all sorts of weird and wonderful creatures, like the Pipe Snake, the Cumulo 5, and even the Island Whale, Hokkaido. The Mushroom Keepers, and especially those from Shikoku, made it their mission to take down these formidable beasts. On top of this, the mushroom bow was a weapon designed specifically to hunt fleeing creatures, so even if Bisco and Milo tried to run, there was no guarantee they would make it.

"We need to break through their ranks," said Milo. "If we can just take out one of them..."

"What?! We can't kill 'em, Milo! That's my tribe!"

"I know you can't do it, Bisco. That's why *I* have to!"

"Milo?! ...Wait, over there!"

The two hit the deck just in time as four Mushroom Keepers jumped out wearing tattered cloaks. Two of them fired arrows at the boys, while the other two took up formation to cut off any escape routes. Thinking quickly, Milo raised his right hand and uttered a simple mantra.

"Shield!"

An emerald wall blocked the two arrows flying their way.

Gaboom!

"Urgh!!"

The arrows exploded into yellow oyster mushrooms, eating away Milo's shield in a flash. Against the Rust-eating properties of the mushrooms, Milo's mantra was all but useless.

Crap!!

The other two archers fired their arrows, fast as a gale. One of them whistled directly toward Milo's throat.

The sound of tearing flesh. A spray of blood.

"Rgh... Huh? Ah...ahhh..."

* * *

Milo felt his partner's weight in his hands. The smell of the sun drifted off his scarlet hair, and Milo's fingers grew slick with his blood. The burning heat of it left him shaking.

"Bisco!!"

"Don't…shoot, Milo…"

The arrow had pierced Bisco's lung. A horrid amount of blood spilled from his lips and onto Milo's chest.

"It don't make it any better…for you to bloody your hands instead. We're one, dumbass. Our karma…and our fate…"

"Aaaaah!! Bisco! Bisco!!" Milo screamed, unable to stop the blood. All he could do was hold his partner close. The regenerative power of the Rust-Eater had always saved Bisco from lesser threats, but his fellow Mushroom Keepers were a force to be reckoned with.

The more powerful a creature, the larger its reserves of vitality, and it was the source of that vitality that Mushroom Keepers aimed for with their strikes. Thus, Bisco's great strength became his downfall, as he was exactly the kind of monster the hunters were trained from birth to defeat.

"Grhh, they got me good. I can't summon up the spores…!"

I need to operate! But…

While Bisco focused on holding back the mushrooms' growth, Milo's mind raced. However, the Mushroom Keepers were not about to show mercy to a wounded foe…

"I ain't feelin' the Rust-Eater no more," one said.

"We've hit him in the cultivator! The next shot'll end it."

"Don't get careless, fellows. Remember, that kid's the strongest Mushroom Keeper alive. Who knows what he's capable of when his life's on the line?"

The hunters moved in cautiously, not dropping their guard for a moment. Milo had few ideas, and very little time to think.

"Stay back!!" he yelled, his sapphire eyes burning like stars. His terrifying glare made the advancing figures pause in their tracks.

I'm a doctor. Protecting life is my mission. It's why I'm here.

"Ain't that the new kid? Where'd all that spirit come from?"

"Don't underestimate him. Remember, he's the man Akaboshi calls his partner. Kill him from a safe distance!"

But to save Bisco…I'll do anything!!

Milo's despair became a beastly rage. He bared his teeth and growled.

"I don't care whose blood I have to spill. I don't care how many of you there are. If anyone takes another step, I'll rip you all to shreds!"

A swarm of mantra cubes materialized in the air around Milo. They spun so fast the hunters' eyes could barely follow as they waited impatiently for Milo's order.

"Don't do it…Milo!!" pleaded Bisco.

"He's casting some kinda spell! Shoot the newbie! Do it now!"

"Won/shandreber/vacurer…"

The Mushroom Keepers drew their bows taut, while Milo, resolve strengthened by Bisco's peril, prepared the most devastating mantra of his life. At the precise moment the two forces seemed poised to wipe each other out, an arrow streaked down from the sky and embedded itself at Milo's feet.

Boom!

"*Sn—* M-mmph?!"

The arrow exploded into what seemed like a giant ball of cotton wool, engulfing the pair. Before the surprised hunters could react, their bows were assaulted by sand velvet mushrooms, breaking the weapons to pieces.

"Wh-what?! What happened to our bows?!"

"It doesn't matter. Bisco's in there! Draw your daggers and finish him off!"

The hostile men descended on the cotton, but before they could reach it, a short-statured Mushroom Keeper burst out of the top, carrying Bisco and Milo in his arms. The man seemed far stronger than his physical size could account for.

"Shikoku folk may be the best around, but y'all youngsters ain't scratch compared to me. You let yerselves get so distracted, you didn't even notice my spores infectin' your bows!"

"*Cough! Cough!* Wh-what just happened?!"

"Hyo-ho-ho!"

Up in the air, his ivory whiskers trailing in the breeze, was a man whose face the two boys had never expected to see.

"Tear 'em all to pieces, you say? Why, my boy, you've got one hell of a mouth on that pretty face!"

""Jabi!!""

"I had to free Actagawa, ya see," the old man said. "So I ran a little late."

"Where have you been?! And how did you get here?!"

"A little birdie showed me the way. See?"

Jabi motioned ahead of him, to the side of an unusually steep cliff. Milo could see something pink hopping up and down in front of a cave entrance.

"Over here! Over here!" the figure cried. "This way, Gramps!!"

""T-Tirol?!""

"If you want the full details, ask the pip-squeak," said Jabi. "I gotta go talk some sense into the young'uns!"

Jabi moved like the wind and landed swiftly by Tirol's side, dropping the blood-soaked pair onto the ground before turning back the way he came.

"Jabi, wait!" said Bisco. "I'm comin', too."

"Like *that*? I don't think so, kid. Let the panda take care of ya," Jabi said, before turning to Milo. "The boy's been hit in the cultivator, laddie. That's spooked the Rust-Eaters, but it ain't as bad as it looks. Remove the arrowhead, and he'll be right as rain."

"O-okay!"

"Are you gonna be all right by yourself, old man?!" shouted Tirol. "Why don't ya stick around until Akaboshi gets better?!"

"You're the one who dragged me out here, lassie! Don't fret—these kids ain't got nothin' on me."

Jabi lifted his hat and fixed the jellyfish-haired girl with a toothy grin.

"Besides, those kids called Bisco the greatest Mushroom Keeper alive, an' I don't recall bein' dead just yet! I'll show 'em who's really top dog around here!"

With that, Jabi leaped back into the sea of dying driftweed. In only three seconds, he had disappeared.

"Get to the back of the cave!" yelled Tirol. "I'm sealin' off the entrance!"

"Are you crazy?!" Bisco shot back. "Jabi's out there fightin' by himself!"

"Once you get yourself healed, you can join him! Fire in the hole!"

Tirol pressed down a lever, and a mighty explosion shook the cave mouth. Falling rocks and stones sealed the way completely. Tirol wiped the sweat from her brow and sighed, her firebeetle lantern now their only source of light.

"Th-thank you, Tirol!" said Milo.

"I bet you got questions for me," she replied. "But right now Aka-bushi comes first. 'Sides, I gotta protect the old man my way."

Milo watched as Tirol took out some sort of boxy portable computer with an integrated display and began tapping away at the keys. Then he turned his attention to Bisco.

"We'll have to skip the anesthetic," he said, unrolling his medical supplies. "It'll interfere with the treatment. Do you think you can bear with it?"

"Who the hell do you think you're talkin' to? Just get me back in the fight, so I can go after Jabi!"

Bisco's eyes were completely fearless. Milo nodded, then selected a sharp metal scalpel and, without hesitation, cut into Bisco's abdomen near the base of the arrow.

It's been a while since I last saw the inside of Bisco's stomach... Oh no! His muscles are too hard; I can't cut through!

Bisco hadn't shown any indication of pain so far, and his breaths were calm and meditative. He was utilizing a technique Jabi had once taught him, shutting out the outside world and focusing his energy to preserve his life for as long as possible. Obviously, this was a technique beyond the reach of most people.

Trying not to let this amazing skill distract him, Milo switched out his scalpel for his trusty lizard-claw knife, plunging it into Bisco's stomach and slitting it open. Inside, Bisco's organs pulsed violently, lighting up the abdominal cavity with an otherworldly golden light. Milo paused. He felt as though he were gazing upon a living universe, each organ a star in the endless void.

…*It's beautiful…*

"…What's up—got the hots for your partner's insides? You're into some freaky shit, Panda Boy."

"D-don't say that! It just surprised me a bit, that's all!!"

Milo anxiously cleared his throat and took another look inside Bisco's body. The tip of the arrow was embedded in a particularly bright organ, which seemed to be preventing the Rust-Eaters from healing him, just as Jabi had said.

Is this the cultivator? What even is it? Where did it come from?

The glowing organ was positioned just above Bisco's liver. Milo had never seen anything like it in all his years slicing up patients. It reminded him of the Ghost Hail Node, the unique organ found in the body of Hokkaido. Milo could only guess that it had grown there some time after Bisco's blood became infused with the Rust-Eater. But if so, he couldn't help marveling at how quickly the transformation had taken place.

Still, Milo couldn't allow this baffling new information to distract him from his job. With practiced ease, he extracted the arrowhead and stitched up Bisco's pierced organ. As soon as he did, the Rust-Eater spores, which had been spilling from the open wound like fireworks, began flowing into Bisco's bloodstream once more.

"Urgh…"

Milo heard Bisco groan and watched as the color slowly returned to his face. Seeing that the procedure had been a success, Milo removed the arrow piercing Bisco's lung as well. As he did so, the wound miraculously healed itself before his very eyes.

"Th-that's it!! It's all over!"

"It's all over? You killed him?" asked Tirol without looking up.

"Like I would ever mess up an operation! Bisco's fine…but he still has to rest. He's lost a lot of blood, and the Rust-Eater is still reproducing it."

"Normally, I'd tell you to just wake him up already," said Tirol, "but I think it's gonna be okay, actually."

"What do you mean?"

"Well…get a load of Akaboshi's pappy. He's toyin' with them. Even I can see that."

Without bothering to clean the blood off himself, Milo left Bisco's side and wandered over to Tirol. It looked like she was using the computer to control her personal drone. The reception was rough, but the screen displayed a staticky view from its camera feed as it scuttled like a spider across the Driftweed Plains.

"You've been following Jabi?"

"Just watch. Here they come!"

The drone turned its gaze upward, and Milo caught sight of three figures jumping overhead. He recognized two of them as the Mushroom Keepers who had attacked him and Bisco, and the third was…

"Jabi! Oh no, watch out!"

Two arrows came flying toward the old man, but just as they were about to skewer him, Jabi stretched and contorted his whole body like a snake, dodging them completely. Then, as if that wasn't shocking enough, he grabbed the two arrows out of the air with nothing but his bare hands.

"Whaaat?!"

"Whoa."

Milo and Tirol were both shocked. Meanwhile, Jabi swung his serpentine body around like a whirlwind, flinging the two arrows back at their owners. They caught the Mushroom Keepers' cloaks, knocking them to the ground, where the arrows exploded into bright-yellow oyster mushrooms.

He's still trying not to kill them!

Jabi's techniques were like the yin to Bisco's yang. While Bisco's arrows were hard-hitting and impactful, his master's were deliberate and precise. Jabi's sharp eyes picked out the Tirol drone, and he called out to it.

"Runnin' low on arrows! Pass me my spares!"

"Here ya go!"

The drone tossed Jabi a fresh quiver, whereupon the old man disappeared once more into the plains like a mist.

"See?" said Tirol, stretching. "Jabi's fine. He don't even need Bisco to— Whoa, Panda, you reek of blood! Even *you'll* turn off the girls smellin' like Freddy Krueger!"

"It was you who went and found Jabi, wasn't it? Thank you, Tirol! You're a lifesaver!"

"Kurokawa was busy followin' you two, and there aren't many people who can fight back... I figured, if there's one guy who can do it, it's him."

Then Tirol muttered, "I'm hungry," and rummaged around in her luggage, pulling out a large bag of green sugar–fried beans. She stuffed a handful into her mouth and began chewing on them.

"How come I always gotta save you guys anyway? I'm gettin' bored of this job. Hurry up and beat Kurokawa so I can switch careers."

"With Jabi on our side, we can't lose! We'll just wait for Bisco to heal up, and then—"

But Milo's newfound optimism didn't last long.

"*Simply amazing! The mushroom master beat fifty of his peers without killing a single one! Not bad for a decrepit old fogy, Jabi!!*"

Kurokawa's voice came through the computer. Tirol jumped and started pressing buttons, panning the drone's camera to a spot above the driftweeds, where Jabi was currently facing off against the Dacarabia.

"Your little game of make-believe ends here, Kurokawa. You've had your fun, stringin' Bisco along for the ride, but now it's time to put down the camera fer good."

"*Heh-heh-heh. Oh, I wouldn't be so sure about that, Jabi.*"

Kurokawa remained defiant in the face of the triumphant Mushroom Keeper.

"That ambush was nothing more than bait to draw you in, and here you are. You're the true focus of this scene, old man."

"What're you yappin' about?"

"Before Obi-Wan's tragic demise, we need the audience to understand his full power! You played the part magnificently, I must say. The fiery bow of the disciple has been utterly outshone by the still water of his master's!"

Kurokawa folded her arms beneath her chest. Her carefree gaze met Jabi's down below, and sparks flew between them like lightning.

"However," she went on. *"It's time to draw this scene to a close, I think. We can't devote too much time to what is, ultimately, only a supporting character."*

Then she switched from her usual mocking tone to something much darker.

"Actors who have played their part must leave the stage."

"Why don'cha just say how you really feel? You want me dead 'cause yer scared of me, that's all!"

"Mmm! Now, that's a one-liner! Aah, just twenty years younger, and you could have been a star..."

Kurokawa smiled—a broad grin that revealed her sharpened teeth. She snapped her fingers, and Pawoo leaped from the craft in a flutter of raven hair. Swinging her staff, she tore apart the driftweeds in her path, closing in on Jabi. The old man kept his eyes fixed on the tip of her weapon, his expression unchanging.

"Will you tear apart a promising young couple for a few more years of life? You know how this has to go, don't you, old man?"

Milo tore his eyes from the display. "Kurokawa's entered the fray!" he yelled. "This is bad. Jabi doesn't have the vaccine yet!"

"But to get outta here, we gotta open the cave!" shouted Tirol. "Where's my blasting kit? I know it's around here somewhere..."

"Out of the way, Tirol!"

Tirol ducked to the side with a yelp just as a scarlet flash from Bisco's bow grazed her braids and embedded itself in the fallen rock.

Gaboom!

There could be no greater demonstration of the red oyster mushrooms' superior power compared to their yellow counterparts. The blast obliterated the fallen rubble in an instant.

"Milo!" Bisco called to his partner. "Let's go!"

"Okay!!"

"Frick, my hair's caught in the... Hey! Don't leave me behind!"

Tirol watched the boys disappear into the wilds like bullets, one of her braids pinned beneath a sizable chunk of displaced rock.

"Bisco!! Are you sure you're okay to fight?" asked Milo.

"It don't matter! Jabi and Pawoo are gonna fight to the death! Even if my heart collapses, I gotta stop them!"

"There they are! Oh no! Pawoo!"

As Milo watched, the Whirling Steel descended on Bisco's aged master like a storm, lashing out mercilessly with her thick iron rod. Jabi's superior skill and experience served him well in predicting Pawoo's blows, but he was clearly fighting a losing battle. Pawoo's forceful swings unleashed heavy blasts of wind that countered Jabi's light, snakelike movements and prevented him from reaching his full potential.

"Hyo-ho-ho! You've got strength, lass! Save some for your husband!!"

"Jabi!" Bisco called out. "Get away! Leave Pawoo to us!!"

"Ah, Akaboshi takes the stage. Let's get a close-up... Hmm? Hold on a second..."

Kurokawa put down the megaphone and sank into thought.

"Now, I know that gorilla can take the two pip-squeaks, but can she handle three at once...?"

"Bisco!! We just need to hold Pawoo back!!" cried Milo.

"Got it!!"

"I shall not let you interfere!!"

Pawoo's deep-blue eyes glowed under the shade of her steel visor as she turned her staff on her husband. Bisco blocked her overhead swing with his bow, but she swiftly followed up with a sideways sweep, and when he blocked this, too, Bisco heard an unsettling creak from his weapon.

"Urgh. My bow can't take much more!"

"Let's switch, Bisco!"

Milo blocked the next swing, taking over for his partner. In his hands was the Lion's Crimson Sword. It glowed gold with the light of the Rust-Eater, having sucked up Bisco's blood off Milo after the operation. In its awakened form, it could block Pawoo's weighty blows without suffering a single nick to the blade.

"Milo! You dare defy your elder sister?!"

"This is an abuse of sibling privilege, Pawoo!"

But Pawoo showed no signs of leniency toward her brother. In fact, if anything, her blows became fiercer and fiercer. Still, with Bisco and Milo able to cover each other's defensive weaknesses, she was finding it difficult to land a decisive blow.

"Grr, this is taking forever!" muttered Kurokawa, watching the fight from the deck of her craft. "Somebody go down and help—"

"D-Director! He's here! We've been boarded!"

"Whaaat?!"

She had only taken her eyes off Jabi for a moment, and yet in that time he had combined his clamshell mushrooms with a wire arrow to catapult his lightweight frame up onto the body of the Dacarabia.

The Immies pointed their rifles skyward. "Shoot him! Don't let him reach the engine— *Gwah!*"

Sweat ran down Kurokawa's neck at the detestable *Gaboom! Gaboom!* sounds coming from above. Suddenly, she heard a different kind of explosion, and a Klaxon began blaring in the cabin as the entire craft pitched forward, slowly falling out of the sky.

"Impossible… He took out the reactor! How is this old coot giving you idiots trouble?! Get up there and fix it!"

"Hyo-ho-ho. Surprised?"

"Grh!"

Kurokawa froze as Jabi's gloating face suddenly appeared upside down outside one of the cabin windows.

"I'll wager this wasn't in your script, eh?! But don't worry— retirement ain't so bad!"

"Director! Watch out...!"

Several rabbit-headed Immie guards jumped out to protect Kurokawa, but Jabi kept blasting them away with his lightning kicks, sending them over the edge to plummet, screaming, into the driftweeds below. Drawing his trusty shortbow, he advanced on Kurokawa, keeping his weapon level.

"Well, you got me," Kurokawa said, smiling. "I didn't plan for this at all. In fact, I was kind of hoping those fifty Mushroom Keepers would do you in. But Akaboshi just had to—"

"Bisco ain't your toy, Kurokawa."

For a moment, Jabi was no longer the doddering fool. His words were like jet-black knives in Kurokawa's mind. He was the one people told stories of: the mad bowman, Akemi Hebikawa.

"Looks like we're both gettin' a one-way ticket to meet the ferryman, kid. We'll have plenty o' time to talk on the boat to hell."

"Y-you..."

Kurokawa gulped.

Then a wide grin spread across her face.

"That's a good look on you, Jabi..."

Shwf!

"Whoopsie-daisy!"

Kurokawa drew her pistol and fired in Jabi's direction, but the old man backflipped out of the way. Then, as soon as Kurokawa appeared in his line of sight once more, he unleashed four different arrows that lodged in a row up Kurokawa's extended arm toward her shoulder.

"Huh?!"

"You still got a few seconds before they bloom. Enough to make your peace, Kurokawa."

"Waaaaahhh! Aaaah...! Aaah...ha! Aaah-ha-ha-haaaa!!"

"!!"

Suddenly, out of nowhere, a flash of light came flying toward Jabi.

He dove to the side, but as if predicting his movement, a second flash rushed toward his new location at supersonic speeds.

Splat!!

"G-ghhgh!!"

"I can't believe you managed to dodge one of them," said Kurokawa leisurely. "What a fearsome old man you are."

One of five long black spikes pierced Jabi's throat and lifted him up into the air. The mysterious weapons were Kurokawa's own fingers.

"But there's something you failed to consider," the dark-eyed woman went on. "I'm a coward. You didn't think I'd appear before Akaboshi with only one gorilla for protection, did you?"

Slurp. Slurp. A black metallic substance coated Kurokawa's injured arm. It pulsated, feeding on the arrows and drawing them into her body.

"Gh...bah... Y-you..."

"Think, you old fool! Wouldn't it make sense that I already had a means of taking Akaboshi on myself?"

Kurokawa retracted her fingers, drawing Jabi closer. Now he could see the full extent of her transformation, and the black steel that covered half her body. It was a person-sized Tetsujin—but this one hadn't been left to rot in the Rust Wind, or reawoken after centuries of disuse. This was the weapon's true form.

"Bisco!! Over there!!" shouted Milo.

"Jabi!!"

"Mrh...!"

Bisco, Milo, and Pawoo paused their battle to stare at the horrifying scene unfolding within the cabin of the descending Dacarabia. Kurokawa, noticing their gazes, gave a little wave and turned her mechanical body for them to admire.

"Sorry to ruin your hopes and dreams, boys, but you know what they say: True beauty is only skin-deep."

"Kurokawa!! Let Jabi go!!"

"I still remember the day you tore my flesh apart with those arrows," said Kurokawa, ignoring the request. "After you put an end to Tetsu-jin, a group of people arrived to take away what remained. The leader of that group was none other than Zenjuro Matoba, the chairman of Matoba Heavy Industries."

"Matoba recovered the Tetsujin?!"

"Their aim, of course, was to see if the weapon could be mass-produced. However, what they didn't know at the time was that a teensy-weensy bit of my mind still inhabited it."

Kurokawa waved her fingers to and fro, flinging Jabi around as she moved.

"One of Matoba's technical advisers was assigned to watch over me, and in an incubation vat, I began my new life as Perfect Tetsujin... I also asked them to make me a woman this time, since that sounded like a lot more fun. But that's beside the point. After I obtained my new body..."

Shwf!!

Bisco wasn't going to listen to another second of Kurokawa's mono-logue. He fired an arrow her way, and although Pawoo jumped in to protect her, Milo blocked her staff with the Lion's Crimson Sword. The red streak barreled through the air unhindered, heading straight for Kurokawa's head.

"Oh, sorry. My story's boring you, is it? Well then, how about this?"

Kurokawa raised her other arm, and a black ripple emanated from her fingertip, creating some kind of force field in front of her. Bis-co's arrow disappeared into the barrier, leaving Kurokawa completely unharmed.

"What?! I missed?!"

Gaboom!!

A second later, a sound came from below—at ground level. Bisco looked down and saw a cluster of bright-red oyster mushrooms sprout-ing from the Driftweed Plains.

"*After Effects*," Kurokawa explained in a low, gritty voice. "A reality-editing tool that allows me to take your arrows and put them somewhere else." She cackled. "You may be divine, Akaboshi, but even you can't stand up to this marvel of twenty-first century engineering! You'll never land a hit on me!"

"Kurokawa…!!!"

"Now do you understand?! I'm the director! I get to exist outside the rules and watch over you forever! And as thanks for putting me here, Akaboshi, I'm going to turn you into the greatest hero who ever graced the silver screen!"

"Rgh! Gh! Gaah!"

"Jabi!"

"Aaand action."

Kurokawa gave a slimy grin, and vines of Rust crept from her fingers. They crawled along Jabi's throat, converging at the back of his neck and culminating in a single Rust flower that suddenly blossomed into existence. Jabi flinched at the violent growth, but then hung his head limply and stopped moving.

"Teacher and student, forced to do battle against their own wishes! Does Bisco have what it takes to strike down his beloved master? …Phew-ee! Sometimes my own genius scares even *me*. Even George Lucas never got a scene like this!"

"Jabi, nooo!!" cried Milo.

"Get back here, Assistant! One of our cameramen was killed; I need you to take over."

Pawoo shot Kurokawa a questioning glance before heading back to the descending Dacarabia. Kurokawa, meanwhile, transformed her arm into a mass of fibers that snaked their way to the craft's engines and brought them back online.

"They're getting away! We need to give Pawoo the vaccine!"

"Wait, Milo!"

There was anger in Bisco's voice as he cut Milo off and took a step forward into the windswept plains, as if to protect his partner. A few meters ahead, a small figure dropped down to face him. The man's silvery whiskers swayed in the breeze, and beneath his tricorne hat lurked a pair of hawkish eyes.

"So, old man, you finally went senile," muttered Bisco through gritted teeth. "Serves you right for lettin' all the fame go to your head. You've gone soft—the Jabi I know would never lose his mind to a couple'a damn tricks!"

"...Hee-hee-hee."

Slowly, Jabi lifted his head. The expression on his face was like nothing Milo had ever seen. It was something he knew only from stories— stories Bisco had told him of the mad bowman, Jabi, who left naught but destruction in his wake.

"You know, sonny..."

The man's tone was just like it had been in his heyday. Bisco broke out in a cold sweat. He remembered that voice.

"...it ain't so bad bein' controlled."

"What?!"

"I gave rise to the world's strongest Mushroom Keeper. That's somethin' I can be proud of."

His cracked lips parted, revealing the gaps in his toothy grin.

"But I can't pass on like this. You understand, don'cha, boy?"

"Spit it out, Jabi! What are you tryin' to say?!"

"We're warriors, son. Both of us."

The fire in the old man's gaze burned a hole straight through Bisco's jade-green eyes.

"For sixty years, I broke down everything in my path. There was nothin' in the world my arrows couldn't pierce...until you showed up."

"..."

"I wanna fight ya, sonny."

"Hrgh...!"

"I wanna see how far my bow'll take me against the world's strongest Mushroom Keeper. You've lit a fire in my heart, boy. Now show me what you got!"

"No, Jabi! Don't do this!"

"Stand back, Milo!!"

Spores blew out from Bisco's body like his skin was boiling, enveloping him in their golden light. Milo just stood there, dumbfounded. He had never seen his partner look so dead serious.

"My old man means business," he said. "It's my job as his disciple to make him eat those words!!"

"Eat my words, hmm? Hee-hee-hee. You're a sweet lad, Bisco."

Shwf!

Bisco nocked an arrow and fired it with supernatural speed. No ordinary human could have dodged his lightning arrow, much less an old man of sixty, but Jabi had the agility of the monkey king himself.

"Still think I'm so sweet, Jabi?!"

"Hee-hee-hee! So sweet I'll lose the rest of my teeth!"

Pchew! Pshoo!

Like a Wild West shootout, the two parties drew their bows and loosed their arrows in perfect unison. Bisco's shot hit Jabi's head-on, and the power of Bisco's superior draw destroyed the opposing arrow completely. However...

"!"

"Silly boy. You think I didn't see that coming, when you've been using the same trick your whole life?"

...Jabi's arrow had been tipped with a scattersoot mushroom for precisely this reason. When Bisco's arrow struck it, it threw up a cloud of smoke that obscured the old man from view. Moments later, three arrows flew out of the cloud and embedded themselves with a series of thuds at Bisco's feet.

"Ha!" Bisco laughed. "I was just checkin' your joints hadn't froze up!"

"Hyo-ho. If I was young again, I'd have you trapped in three more moves!"

"Yeah? Well, unlike you, I'm still learnin' new tricks!"

Bisco clenched his teeth and drew his bow back as far as he could, loosing a golden arrow at the source of the smoke. An enormous Rust-Eater exploded into being, and the burst of spores blew the soot away.

"Hyo-ho-ho!" laughed Jabi, pressing his hat to his head before the force of the mushroom's awakening blew it clean off. "You never did have a soft touch. You really need all that power just to defeat one little old man?"

"Quit yammerin' before I save your dentist some trouble!"

Bisco fired more and more Rust-Eater arrows into the earth, their long stalks stretching upward after Jabi. But the old man kept weaving and leaping between them, never allowing one to hit.

"Dammit! He's as slippery as ever!"

"...Oh no! Bisco!" cried Milo. "Stop firing!"

"Huh?!"

Distracted by Jabi's flitting movements like a bull by a matador's cape, Bisco failed to notice what the old man was doing before it was too late. The Rust-Eaters Bisco had fired began changing color, their caps becoming dark as coal.

"The hell?! What's happening to the Rust-Eaters?!"

"He's rewritten the mushrooms!" Milo cried, eyes wide with wonder. "Jabi fired his scattersoot mushrooms into your Rust-Eaters, replacing them with his own! Just how skilled in the mushroom arts is he?!"

"He did what?!"

The golden stalks went dark before his very eyes, like storm clouds passing over the sun. Bisco felt himself break into a cold sweat. In all his years studying under Jabi, he'd never seen him use this technique before.

"I may have been your teacher, but I'm still a Mushroom Keeper, boy, and a Mushroom Keeper never reveals his hand!"

"Hrh! There you are!"

Bisco turned and loosed an arrow, swift as lightning, in the direction of Jabi's voice, but the new scattersoot mushrooms had already cloaked the area in darkness, and Bisco could barely see the tip of his own nose. Jabi had succeeded in turning Bisco's overwhelming life force to his own advantage.

"I can't see a thing!" cried Milo. "Bisco, use your goggles!"

"I am, but it ain't workin'! Jabi ain't showin' up!"

"He's not showing up? But how?!"

"He musta used a mortishroom to lower his own body temperature!" Bisco shouted back. "Only my old man would do somethin' so— Grrrh!"

From out of the darkness came a single arrow, speeding through the air and landing solidly in Bisco's leg. The master archer had put a spin on it, lending it enough penetrative power so that even Jabi's waning strength could deliver it through Bisco's hardened muscle.

"Bisco!! You can't give up!"

"Goddammit... You crazy old man!!"

I need to hit that flower on Jabi's neck with the Rust flower vaccine. But how, when Jabi's so strong?!

The two boys fled aimlessly through the smoke, but Jabi was simply toying with them. He fired a couple more arrows, which found their marks in Bisco's shoulder and arm. Bisco grunted through the pain, trying to turn his grief into anger.

"B-but how?!" exclaimed Milo. "How can Jabi see where we are?!"

"How can I not?" came the old man's voice. "It's like lookin' directly into the sun! I couldn't miss ya if I wanted to! Have ya really grown so weak you didn't even realize that?"

"Goddammit, if only we knew where he— Urghh!"

"Bisco!!"

Another arrow planted itself in his thigh, and Bisco fell to his knees at last. Milo wrapped his arms around him, trying desperately to protect him from any more unseen attacks.

For a short while, all was silent. Then a low, dark voice issued from within the smoke.

"...You disappoint me, laddie. The power o' the divine only made you weaker."

"Weaker...?!" Bisco's eyes trembled as a bead of sweat dripped down his back. "You think I've grown weaker?!"

The voice from the darkness lashed out at his pupil's denial. "You have. Used to be, you put your life on the line each time you took up the bow. Not anymore."

This was neither the doddering old fool nor Bisco's fiendish master. This was the voice of a mad warrior, concerned with strength alone.

* * *

"You've prayed too much for the world, Bisco, and you've forgotten to pray for yourself. You're so addicted to helping people that you forgot you're nothing but an arrow. You've grown stale, boy. How can I make you remember your true self? Gouge out your eyes? Cut off your ears? …Or maybe this'll do the trick…"

Pshoo!
The sound of Jabi's bow came from behind. Bisco braced himself for the inevitable impact.
Splat!
"…Huh? G-guhh…!"
"Milo!!"
Jabi's arrow had skimmed Bisco's ear and penetrated Milo's neck in a splatter of blood. Milo pressed one hand over his throat to stop the bleeding, and in spite of his fading consciousness, rummaged around among the needles at his waist. Just as he picked out a lurkershroom medicine, however, another arrow impaled his hand, breaking the vial and scattering its contents.
"Aaaagh!!"
"Milo!!" Bisco's eyes ran red with fury. "Leave him alone, Jabi, or I swear I'll tear you apart!!"
"It's all…his fault."
Bisco drew his dagger and sliced apart another arrow moments before it reached Milo's skin. However, no sooner had he done that than two more arrows came flying in from a different direction, hitting Milo in the hip and thigh.
"Gggahh!!"
The doctor's scream sounded as if it might rip apart his throat.
"It's all his fault," came Jabi's voice. "Because of him, you have every-thin' you need! I gotta kill him, so you'll remember the way you used to thirst!"
"Stop it, Jabi! This ain't right! I don't wanna have to kill you! …You're my old man!"

"You're weak! Weak, weak, weak! You ain't a god, Bisco! You ain't a devil! You're an arrow! And there's only one thing arrows are meant to do!"

Jabi unleashed a hail of shots, and while Bisco could still dodge, Milo was in no state to do so. The arrows perforated him like a pincushion, leaving him unable to even speak, for the blood clogging his throat.

"Bis...co...," he gurgled.

"Milo!! Keep it together!!"

"Stay with me..."

Milo collapsed into Bisco's arms, fully aware of his own impending death. As he felt his partner's warm blood on his hands, Bisco's eyes gleamed with a terrifying light. Raw determination blossomed in his heart like a mushroom, wiping away all hesitation.

His light was noble and pure, ready to stake it all on a single arrow—for the one he couldn't allow to be taken from him.

"Now it's time to finish you off," came Jabi's voice.

Archery...is two things.

Bisco took a deep breath and pulled back on the bowstring. The two boys' blood mingled and soaked into the arrow's feathers.

No... Only one thing matters!

In response to Bisco's fierce will, the mixture of their blood began to glow. Starting from the fletching and working its way up, the light engulfed the entire shaft in a prismatic, multicolored glow. These were the miracle spores that Bisco's body had been able to produce on only one prior occasion. The rainbowshroom.

"Hngaaaah..."

"!!"

Through the soot-black smoke, Jabi saw the light of Bisco's hair, like an aurora flickering in the night sky.

Here it comes!

Jabi smiled giddily at the transformation taking place.

Here it comes! I'm about to witness a monster!

He drew his bow, but no longer simply to torment the pair. Now his weapon was filled with purpose, as though its arrow contained all his remaining life.

* * *

I knew I would have to resort to this, Bisco. This technique, the Soulprint Arrow, *only works on foes stronger than the user. My craving drives its path. It will never stop chasing you so long as I will it!*

Kurokawa's Rust flower augmented Jabi's strength. The vines crawled up his arms and across the arrow, pulsing ominously.

"All that remains of my life...I stake on this single shot!"

In the darkness, Bisco closed his eyes.

Archery...the soul of archery is simply...
 ...to believe.

His partner rested softly against his chest. All Bisco could feel was his warmth.

"It's time to settle this, Bisco!"

Believe...
 Bisco thought of nothing but Jabi. With eyes closed tight, he fired.

Pchew!!
 Pshoo!!

Bisco's rainbow arrow glistened like a smattering of diamonds.
 But it missed its target by a long shot.
 Jabi's arrow, meanwhile, flew on a perfect trajectory toward the center of Bisco's forehead.

I...I won!
 A flawless victory.
 ...Or so Jabi thought. But as he watched, he couldn't help but sweat, as though poised on the verge of a hundred deaths.

My arrow was perfect! he thought. *My entire life's work! However he tries to dodge, the* Soulprint Arrow *will hunt him down!*

The arrow, infused with the Rust flower, didn't so much as tremble as it swept through the air, piercing the darkness on an unstoppable path to Bisco's skull.

This is good-bye, Bisco!

And then, just as it reached its target...

...it stopped.

"...Wh-what?!"

It hung impossibly for a moment in midair before gravity took over and Jabi's ultimate arrow clattered to the ground.

"Th-the *Soulprint Arrow*! That ain't possible!"

"You lost faith," muttered Bisco, resolute. "Just for a moment, you didn't think you could win."

"...Shut up!!"

Pchew! Pchew! Pchew!

Jabi hid his astonishment behind a flurry of arrows. He spun like a gale, releasing projectiles in all directions. All of them curved to meet their target, and all of them froze and dropped to the ground mere centimeters before Bisco's head.

"...This can't be happening! How?!"

It was impossible. It defied reality, physics, and common sense. Jabi felt a power much larger than himself wash over him, and he shivered with fright.

"The *Soulprint Arrow* can't ever miss," he said through ragged breaths. "You musta done something! Some new trick or power I ain't never seen before!"

Bisco rose to his feet, his rainbow hair swaying in the wind.

"I didn't do anything, Jabi. I just had faith."

A single tear ran down his tranquil face.

"I believed. Just like you taught me."

Jabi couldn't take his eyes off Bisco's expression. This was the face of his loyal student from all those years ago. He allowed it to distract him, just for a moment...

Fwoosh!

The soot smoke parted as a rainbow-colored streak passed through on its way to Jabi. A startled cry escaped his lips as he realized what it was. It was the very arrow Bisco had fired a few moments ago. Like a flash, Jabi pointed his bow at the ground, releasing a cluster of clamshell mushrooms that propelled him back into the air and out of the arrow's path.

"The *Soulprint Arrow*?! No, this is… Nrgh?!"

As Jabi tracked the arrow with his eyes, its motion shocked him a second time. A short fraction of a second after it missed him, the rainbow arrow changed direction, switching back in midair like a bird of prey and dispelling the dark clouds of soot. Jabi fired leadshrooms one after the other in an attempt to block the arrow's path, but the rainbow streak shattered them all without slowing down.

"…No! This ain't the *Soulprint Arrow*! It's…something else!"

Jabi's eyes sparkled, enraptured by the sight.

"It ain't just changin' direction; that arrow's destined to hit me! There ain't a force on earth that can stop it!"

Jabi jumped up into the now clear air, avoiding Bisco's miracle arrow for as long as possible.

"Hyo-ho-ho! I ain't never seen nothin' like it! He changed the rules, just by thinkin' about it! Bisco's faith rewrote the world!"

He was happy, smiling like a child. He looked down at Bisco, meeting the boy's pleading gaze.

"I call it the '*Ultrafaith Arrow*,' Bisco! Well done! I have to admit, you got me beat! Or no…'cause I taught you everythin' you know, I guess it counts as my win! Hyo-ho-ho!"

"Jabi!! No, don't go!!"

Perhaps Bisco already knew. The Rust flower had ingrained itself too deeply. This conversation with his master would be Bisco's last.

"It's not fair!" Bisco yelled. "Don't leave! You gave me everythin', and I never got a chance to repay you!"

"You just did, sonny! Nothing could make me prouder than seein' my kid surpass his old man!"

Jabi smiled, the wrath exorcised from his face. Then he readjusted his hat before delivering his final words.

"Bisco, my boy! We were the greatest!"

Thudd!

Framed against the moon, Bisco's rainbow arrow pierced Jabi's silhouette.

Bisco didn't look away. His jade-green eyes quivered as he burned the scene into his mind, watching his master fall to earth like an injured swan. All the rage and pain threatened to drive him mad. It was at that moment that someone placed their arms around him.

It was Milo. In the new world Bisco's arrow had created, he was fully healed. Wordlessly, he clung to Bisco's shoulder, catching the emotion that poured from his partner's heart like water from a brimming cup.

Bisco watched the wind beat his master's cloak where his body lay on the ground, never looking away. His trembling hand found the back of Milo's sky-blue head and clutched it tightly.

"Hey, what's going on down there?! Nobody told me that old fart was going to use scattersoot mushrooms! The cameras can't see a damn thing!"

Kurokawa sat in the Dacarabia's cabin, no longer even attempting to conceal her mechanical body. With the thumb of her right hand transformed into a film camera, she gazed through it at the battlefield below.

"We have cat-eye lenses. If we fix those to the cameras, then…"

"Whoa, whoa, whoa. You think we're filming some experimental art piece here?! We need clear footage! Besides, that crazy coot fired a mortishroom into himself, so even the thermals won't pick him— Huh?!"

Kurokawa watched in shock as the scattersoot spores faded and Jabi leaped out of the dark into the sky.

"!"

Pawoo felt a strong wave of power wash over her body and looked up.
"Director," she said. "We must retreat. I sense…a disturbance. Some
great power we have yet to experience."

"Well, that's exactly what we're here to see! Surely you're not suggest-
ing we pack up and leave?"

"You could die, Director. The film cannot continue without you."

"Bullshit! Our leading man is down there risking his life! The least I
can do is— Wh-what the…?! Look!!"

Suddenly, there was a brilliant flash of rainbow light, and a shimmering streak pierced the old man. Kurokawa managed to get the
exact moment on camera.

"Whoa?! Wh-what just happened?" said Kurokawa, greatly agitated.
"Was that Akaboshi? Did he kill him? I—I can't believe we got that!"

Pawoo, meanwhile, ran over to the windows and gazed out, her
indigo eyes quivering beneath her skullcap.

…*Master Jabi…!!*

"Hmm, I double-checked the footage, and I still don't get it. It looks
like an arrow…but it doesn't move like one. It keeps bending around.
Did Nekoyanagi do that with his magic?"

"Director! Look!"

An Immie assistant pointed a finger outside, and when Kurokawa
saw what he was pointing to, she leveled the camera at once.

It was Bisco, his master's lifeless body under one arm, supported on
the other side by his partner, Milo. He was just standing there, glaring
at the Dacarabia.

Pawoo snatched her staff and prepared to protect Kurokawa against
an attack, but as soon as she looked into Bisco's eyes, she found herself
arrested, as if by some mysterious force, unable to utter a word.

"…Oh, Akaboshi. That look…," murmured Kurokawa, intoxicated.
Even with all the rage and despair swirling around within his heart,
Bisco Akaboshi's face held only fierce resolve. He had taken the storm
inside himself and made it part of his infinite determination. The boy's
noble gaze struck Pawoo so deeply, it seemed for a moment she might
break free of Kurokawa's subjugation.

"A boy, standing tall in the wilderness… Oh, it gives me the shivers. No one else could see you the way I do. No one else could capture the truth on film. We're approaching the final scene, Akaboshi. And I'm counting down the seconds…"

As if struck by Bisco's mighty gaze, Kurokawa's emotions spilled forth. No mockery, only the truth. Then she put away her camera, took out her megaphone, and bellowed down at the two boys.

"Akaboshi! The scene is set! The table laid! The final act will take place in Imihama, back where it all began!"

The wind rolled across the plains and whistled through their hair. Two jade-green eyes and a pair of jet-black pits called out to each other across the void.

Kurokawa turned off the megaphone. "…I'll be waiting, Akaboshi," she said. "I love you."

The Dacaiabia turned and flew off toward distant Imihama, leaving only the two boys, windswept and alone beneath the starry sky.

"Is this some kind of joke?! What kind of hack editing is this?! We had much better shots. Why didn't you use those?!"

"W-well, they all have you in-frame, Director…"

"Then edit me out! What do you think the CGI department is for?!"

"Eeep…!"

The Imihama Prefectural Bureau had been transformed into a giant editing studio. Rows of desktop computers filled the space, with industrious editor Immies tapping away at the keys. Their equipment was brand-new, but the cardboard boxes it came in were all they had for chairs. Everywhere, Immies cried out in pain and rubbed their aching backs.

"Chop, chop!" yelled Kurokawa. "We have to tie up the rest of the movie before Akaboshi arrives! Otherwise, I won't know how to shoot the final scene!"

"W-we can't! The machines are at their limit!" one Immie cried. "Any faster, and the rendering cores will overheat!"

"Then cool them down! Wrap your bodies around them and draw away the heat! Don't forget, we're making a masterpiece here! Sacrifices are part of the process! The next time I hear the words 'can't,' 'limit,' or 'impossible,' you're all fired!"

Kurokawa stood before a large screen, urging the workers on. Sweat dripped down her chest, and she boldly unfastened her top and began fanning herself with her megaphone.

"Hee-hee-hee… Oh, this film is gonna go down in history…"

A pointy-toothed grin spread over Kurokawa's face, and she tossed aside her thirty-sixth empty bottle of grape Fanta. As soon as the repurposed wine bottle shattered on the ground…

Ka-boom!!

…a tremendous explosion rocked the foundations of the building, and the sound of a Klaxon filled the room. The Immies looked at one another in confusion, but Kurokawa only smiled.

"He's here. Where did that come from?!"

"Fourth floor, west wing! They're destroying the equipment store-rooms as they go!"

"Pawoo! I have some final checks to take care of. Go greet our guests, will you?"

"As you wish."

Pawoo shot out of the room like a gale. Kurokawa watched her go, then turned to the screen behind her, which featured a shot from the film's penultimate scene. Bisco stared intently into the camera, the body of his fallen master in his arms.

"Our lead has already given so much…we cannot allow this film to fail. I will oversee the final scene personally."

At last, the screen went black, displaying the words FINAL EDITING COMPLETE. Then one of the nearby tape decks popped open, revealing the movie's master reel. Kurokawa stood up out of her chair and was about to collect it when a pink-colored Immie placed her hand on Kurokawa's shoulder, gently sitting the governor back down.

"Don't trouble yourself, Director. I'll get it."

"Hmm? Oh, thank you. How kind."

Kurokawa watched the short-statured Immie wander over toward the tape deck.

"…Hmm?" she said aloud. "I don't remember one like that on the staff…"

The pink Immie arrived at the machine, picked up the completed film reel, cast a shifty glance from side to side…then bolted for the studio door.

"...Huh?"

Kurokawa wasn't sure what had happened at first. As the truth began to dawn on her, she felt the hairs at the back of her neck prick up.

"...S-somebody stop her! Thief! Movie burglar! She snatched my film!"

"Director! Assistant Director Pawoo will make contact with the intruders shortly!"

"Who cares?! That girl just stole the masters! What are you doing?! Go after her!"

But none of the staff listened to Kurokawa's impassioned plea. They were all so engrossed in their work that they couldn't spare an ear. Not even the slam of the studio door roused a single one from their workaholic trance, and Kurokawa kicked her chair in frustration before heading for the door alone.

"Who dares steal my tape? That's my life's work!"

As she moved, her iron legs transformed into the powerful limbs of Tetsujin itself. She flung a heel at the weighty iron door of the studio, delivering such a devastating kick that it flew off its hinges and down the hallway.

"Eeeep!"

The door snagged one of the pink Immie's ears, pulling off the mask and revealing four pink braids that bounced as the girl ran.

"I should have known it was you, Jellyfish!" roared Kurokawa. "I thought you'd help bring me Jabi, so I spared your life, and this is how you repay me?! You're meddling with my magnum opus!"

"Magnum opus? I'd rather watch an ant colony live-feed than this snoozefest!"

"Arm cannons!"

Kurokawa raised her right hand, and there was a *Boom! Boom!* as the integrated cannon fired, blasting apart the walls and floors. Tirol was tossed this way and that by the explosions, but always managed to land on her feet like a cat, and never stopped running.

Kurokawa growled. "Of all the...! Akaboshi's right here in the building, and I'm missing it! I need that tape!!"

Tirol disappeared into one of the many doors lining the hallway. Kurokawa walked up to it and once again kicked it off its hinges before stepping inside.

"Storeroom Number Three? Where are you, Jellyfish?! Show yourself!"

The room inside was large and full of dust. Kurokawa peered around in the darkness, when suddenly there was a *Bam! Bam!* from overhead as the lights came on.

"?!"

"Heh. Led you right here, sucker."

There, atop a mountain of steel crates, sat Tirol. Her nose was bleeding, but the golden glimmer in her eyes was as strong as ever.

"One year! One whole year of lickin' boots and livin' in the worst city on earth! Did you never wonder what I was up to this whole time?"

"You think I care who you've been screwing behind my back, you little whore?"

"Oh, you'll wanna know this!"

A concert of whirring noises rose up from all corners of the storeroom. Then dozens of pairs of crimson pinpricks appeared in the darkness. Slowly, their owners stepped into the light.

"Wh-what are they?!"

"Lightweight Mokujin, Tirol-Ones!" shouted Tirol, wiping her bloody nose. "I been workin' on 'em every day for the last year! Even you can't handle thirty of 'em!"

At Tirol's command, the pink Mokujin attacked. Their left arms transformed into cannons and fired upon the evil director from all angles.

"Aaaaaagh!"

Kurokawa attempted to protect herself, but the cannon blasts tore apart her clothes and flesh, revealing the machine beneath.

"Those were my best clothes, you brat. And those thighs were to die for!" Kurokawa's face became a twisted mask of rage. "You worm… Have your fun, because in three more seconds, it'll all be over."

"Tsk. This ain't workin'. Get in there and beat her to a pulp, Tirol-Ones!"

The Mokujin transformed their cannon arms into crowbars and launched themselves at Kurokawa, but...

Bang! Bang! Bang!

...a series of gunshots rang out. Six Tirol-Ones were struck.

"*Agaric Magnum*...direct hit."

Gaboom! Gaboom!

The struck Mokujin were torn apart by bright-red mushrooms that grew from their circuits. Two large, bulky pistols sat in Kurokawa's hands. She spun them, and the spent shell casings clattered to the floor.

"What the hell?! A mushroom gun?!"

"Is that the end of your little scene?" Kurokawa jeered. "A shame. I would have liked to—"

"Don't stop!" Tirol yelled. "Turn her into scrap metal!"

"H-hey, wait!"

The other Mokujin all took their crowbars and began beating Kurokawa over the head with them. Her face turned redder and redder in indignation.

There was a *Click!* as she reloaded her twin magnums. "Don't... interrupt...me...while I'm gloating!!"

Bang! Bang! Gaboom! Gaboom!

Kurokawa fired into the swarming Tirol-Ones, sending them flying back. The toadstools shredded their engines, scattering parts and machinery around the room. A stray screw scratched Tirol's cheek, drawing blood, and she scowled.

"Damn. All this, and it still ain't enough to beat her?"

Kurokawa blew at the smoke rising from her magnum pistols. "I'm impressed you managed to get this old scrap moving again," she sneered, "but at the end of the day, these are nothing but mass-produced fakes. My power is Tetsujin's power, combined with a miracle of modern science: me. Even a hundred wouldn't stand a chance."

"It ain't over yet! I can still—"

"It's time for you to leave the limelight, you ham actress."

Gaboom!

Toadstools exploded behind Tirol and blasted her off the pile of crates, sending her rolling along the floor until Kurokawa's heel stopped her.

"Now, the tape, if you please. And careful—it's delicate."

"Grrr…!"

Since Tirol was unwilling to part with the goods, Kurokawa grabbed her fingers. There was a sickening *Crakk!*

"Grrrraahhh!!"

"You've wasted enough of my time, girl. Seriously, I throw you a bone, and this is the thanks I get? No amount of book smarts will change what you are, I'm afraid. Go back to selling your body on the street—it's what you're good at."

"Grrh… Fuck, my phalanges…!"

Tirol clutched her bent fingers and scowled up at Kurokawa through tears. Kurokawa rolled her eyes and slammed a heel into Tirol's face, breaking her nose.

"Gyah!"

The force of the kick nearly knocked Tirol out. Kurokawa bent over and lifted the girl by her braids.

"Now… What were you planning to do, stealing this tape? It's hardly the most valuable thing around here."

"…"

"Answer me. I have a torture scene I'm workshopping, you know, and I don't mind using you to test it out."

"…Kheh-heh-heh."

"Hmm…?"

Half of Tirol's face was stained with blood, and yet she wore a defiant smile.

"Planning? Ya got it all wrong. My part's already done. Heh. Look at ya, all proud of yourself for breakin' some cheap dolls. Can't wait to tell the others about this when I get to hell…"

"You worm!"

Kurokawa transformed her other arm into a spear, but just as she held it over her target, poised to strike...

"Oh, Director. There you are."

"One moment, please," said Kurokawa without turning around. "I'll be right with you after I exterminate this pest. You all find Pawoo and... Hmm? That voice..."

Kurokawa began to turn around, but before she could...

Slice!!

...there was a flutter of blue hair, a glimmer of steel, and the arm she was using to hold Tirol was lopped off. The assailant sent Kurokawa reeling and followed up with a spinning kick to her throat, delivered with all the grace and precision of a *naginata* blade.

"Grrrh?!"

Kurokawa hit the wall hard and looked up just in time to see dozens of stacked crates toppling down on her. After watching to make sure she didn't get back up, the newcomer darted over to Tirol.

"Tirol!! Oh no, there's blood everywhere! Tirol, stay with me!"

"Urgh... What took you so long, Panda?!"

"I'm sorry! But I got Bisco and Pawoo face-to-face, and it's all thanks to you for distracting Kurokawa!"

"You'd better be payin' my hospital fees! That'll be a million sols, you know!"

Tirol smiled. Milo hugged her tight, before drawing his dagger and approaching the spot where Kurokawa lay.

"How long do you plan to keep this up, Kurokawa?" he said. "You're no actor."

"...Hee-hee-hee..."

Kurokawa's laughter could be heard from beneath the crates.

"I see, it was all a ploy," she said, "and I fell for it hook, line, and sinker. But are you sure Akaboshi can undo Pawoo's brainwashing by himself? The Rust flower connects to its victim via the spinal column. There's no way to shoot it without killing the host."

"You're awfully cocky for someone who died once already," Milo shot back, unperturbed by Kurokawa's words. "Bisco's faith is enough to change reality. He doesn't have to dance to your tune anymore!!"

"Well, you sure have hyped him up. I can't wait to…see!!"

A jet-black spear shot out from between the boxes toward Milo, but quick as a flash, he swung his lizard-claw blade, knocking the spear aside and cutting the tip clean off.

"Still resorting to sneak attacks?" said Milo. "You'll have to be smarter than that. I'm not the same naive little boy I was in Imihama!"

"Oh, I know that," Kurokawa said, grinning. "Keep watching."

The severed spearhead flew across the room and hit one of the broken Tirol-Ones, covering it in a cobweb of dark vines. This ivy then spread to the other Mokujin, turning their bodies as black as coal.

Milo gasped.

"Th-that freak, she's doin' somethin' to my robots!"

"Tee-hee-hee-hee. Just a little reprogramming. All these Mokujin are now under my command. I'll teach you what happens to those who get in my way!"

After blasting away the crates, Kurokawa stepped into the light once more. Half her body and face had peeled away, revealing the jet-black body of the Perfect Tetsujin beneath. One eye glowed an ominous red.

"I'm glad you're here, too," she said to Milo. "Now I get to kill you both! I can't stand sneaky little know-it-alls who think they're so smart just because they managed to pull one over on me!"

"Well, I did also go to school."

"So did I, shithead! Now die to my *Director Cannon!*"

Kurokawa's arm transformed into a megaphone-shaped rocket launcher, and she unleashed a shot that shook the whole room. Milo grabbed Tirol and leaped aside, letting the cannon blast a hole in the side of the building.

"M-Milo! How the hell are we supposed to win against that?!"

"Hmm, I don't think we can."

"Wh-whaaat?!"

"At least, not alone. Let's go!"

Milo picked up Tirol and jumped out of the hole into the night sky
· above Imihama. Kurokawa, who had been expecting a counterattack
and still had her shield up, cocked her head.

"Huh? ...Th-they're getting away! After them!"

The reprogrammed Mokujin streamed out of the hole one after the
other, while Kurokawa activated her leg boosters and jetted into the
night in hot pursuit.

* * *

Pawoo Nekoyanagi, the Steel Cyclone. Her staff was said to be a hurri-
cane that shredded everything it touched. However, the true nature of
this fierce technique was surprisingly gentle.

Pawoo was dedicated to nonlethal combat, avoiding killing her enemies wherever possible. Honed with the aim of protecting her brother
and all good people of the land, her technique allowed Pawoo to eradi-
cate evil without harming anyone besides the truly evil.

By saving lives, I suppress the demon within.

Sooner or later, all masters had to run up against their inner brutality. It was through this dialogue that Pawoo came to the following
conclusion:

My staff is the staff of life... And that is why I will never best Bisco.

The *Clack, Clack* of her heels rang out against the linoleum floor.

*My staff delivers the one life amid a hundred deaths. Bisco will spot that
and seize it like a hawk; it's how he's survived all these years.*

And yet never have I been so grateful for this technique as I am today.

*For I could receive no higher honor than to fall in battle against my
beloved husband.*

Pawoo strode through the halls of the bureau. The Rust flower had
taken root deeply at the top of her spine, and dark vines extended

outward from it. The last remaining vestiges of her sanity breathed a sigh of relief as she arrived before the door to her fate.

"Hi-yah!!"

Boom! Boom!

With two perpendicular swings of her staff, Pawoo shredded the heavy iron door. In the room beyond lay a dozen Immies, sprawled out across the floor. And at the other side of them, atop the pile of rubble his mushroom arrows had made of the exterior wall, sat the redheaded rogue himself.

"Yo," he said, but he didn't look at her. He was busy struggling with a bag of chips that one of the Immies had been carrying. Despite the big letters on one side reading OPEN HERE, it appeared not to yield to anything the boy tried.

"Still having trouble with those?" Pawoo asked. "Give it here. I'll do it."

"Don't make fun of me... There! Got it!"

Eventually, the bag burst open, revealing that the contents had been completely pulverized by Bisco's attempts. The boy seemed unbothered by this and poured the dust into his mouth before tossing the empty bag aside.

"Been waitin' for this," he said, with a mouth full of food. "Ready to throw down?"

"Bisco," said Pawoo. "Perhaps you know this already, but the Rust flower has spread its roots deeply. It can no longer be removed through normal means."

"Hmm..."

"Once this fight begins, your life shall be in my hands. I will use everything in my power to destroy you."

"No, you won't."

Bisco swallowed the last of the chip dust and wiped his mouth, before descending from his throne of rubble and looking Pawoo directly in the eye.

"You're a shitty liar, unlike your brother," he said. "It's obvious as all hell that you came here to die."

"..."

"Jabi said it, too… That it wasn't so bad bein' controlled. Now you can be closer to your husband than ever before."

"What do you mean by that?!"

"Since we got married, there's been a weird barrier between us. But now that you're brainwashed, you can smash it down."

Pawoo's eyes trembled, but Bisco's were as firm as iron.

"For the next three minutes, you don't have to lie to yourself anymore. Come at me like you mean to kill me, Pawoo!"

Bisco's spirit exploded in a gust of wind that made their hair leap and flutter. His jade-green eyes twinkled with a mixture of fierce determination and utmost trust.

"K-kill you?!" repeated Pawoo.

"You know, I always respected how you could fight without killin'. But you've been holdin' yourself back. You've never fought at your full potential."

"B-but…!"

"I've never seen the real you, underneath it all. I've failed at bein' your husband. I hate to admit it, but I know when I need to own up."

By now, Bisco's cheeks were bright red, but he filled his lungs with air, turned toward Pawoo, and did something unbelievable. The man who acquiesced to nothing but the gods bowed as deeply as he could.

"I'm sorry," he said.

"D-do you have any idea what you're asking?!" Pawoo yelled, voice aquiver. "Even if I am doomed to fail, you ask me to seek your life! To unleash the demon within and slay my beloved husband!"

"If I can't handle you at your worst…," Bisco replied, "…then I don't deserve you! I'd have no right to call you my wife!"

Those words drove a spike through Pawoo's heart. Something inside her began to collapse. Despite Bisco's abnormal moral compass and absurd understanding of marriage, something within his words struck her deeply.

I want…him.

The man I love…

I want him to defeat me!!

Her fingers curled tightly around her metal staff, her teeth clenched and ground together, and the very air around her strained.

I want to fight. Without bonds or chains. Without duty or law. Completely unfettered, as I truly am.
And I want him to destroy it all!!

Pawoo found herself panting like a starved wolf, holding herself back from the strange ecstasy and wild rage building up inside her.

No, no, no! I can't lose myself; that's the antithesis of everything I strive for! It's the Rust flower, driving me to do something I don't want to do!

"Pawoo!"

Bisco's clear voice brought her out of her daze. She looked up into his burning eyes.

"Do you really not trust me? Do you really think I'm that weak? Well?!"

He flew at her—so blindingly fast that the sound of his foot leaving the floor reached her only after he did. Pawoo moved before she could think. Her sleek raven hair rose like a nest of rearing vipers, and her expression was that of the ice queen, a face she'd forsaken long ago.

"Biscooo!!"

Boom!!

Pawoo's staff came down with zero hesitation and enough force to shatter Bisco's skull. The redheaded rogue dodged the blow by the breadth of a single one of his spiky hairs and flashed her a daring grin.

"Hah!" he said. "Now that's more like it! It's gonna be tough to get through that guard!"

"I held it in for so long!" yelled Pawoo, through teary eyes and between devastating swings. "I swore a vow to protect you, to be modest and virtuous! Now that you've seen the real me, there's no going back!!"

Pawoo's long hair fell across her face, and behind those inky coils her eyes burned like those of some vengeful fiend. The light within them was Pawoo's very soul, an inseparable mixture of murder, excitement, and uncontainable pleasure.

Oh, wow. She's even more strung out than I'd thought...

"You must accept it all, Bisco!!"

Bam!! Clang!!

Bisco caught her powerful swing on the side of his bow. His muscles screamed out in protest, and his hand dropped to the dagger at his belt, but...

"Hi-yaaah!!"

...the opposite end of Pawoo's staff came round and slammed Bisco in the side. Pawoo had spun the weapon 360 degrees around her body to attack Bisco in his unguarded spot. Not even a sound betrayed its supersonic speed.

"Grugh?!"

Bisco groaned as the impact shattered his rib cage and sent him hurtling into the storeroom wall in a cloud of dust.

Pawoo stood there, panting and using her staff for support. She wanted to jump in and finish him off, but her body was too exhausted.

"...The forbidden technique, *Snakebite*!"

Pawoo's staff technique was meant to disable the foe in a single blow, so follow-up strikes were not normally part of her repertoire. However, unfettered as she was now, it was only a matter of unleashing her full power on the reverse swing. The toll on Pawoo's muscles was considerable, but the *Snakebite* was meant to be unblockable and impossible to survive.

However...

Bisco will not die so easily! Come on, stand!

Sweat drenched Pawoo's face as she watched the spot where Bisco had fallen, fire in her eyes. Then, just as the strength returned to her legs, an arrow flew from the dust.

"There it is!!"

Boom!

Pawoo's lightning-fast swipe caught the tip of the arrow and, with incredible control, rotated the projectile so that it shot back toward its master.

You took me by surprise before, but now I can read you like a book!

Then Pawoo's powerful thighs launched her into the air, cracking the ground at her feet. She would take advantage of Bisco's moment of weakness.

"Die with me, Bisco!!"

"I knew you could do it, Pawoo..."

"Huh?!"

"I knew you could deflect that shot back at me!!"

Gaboom!

The mushroom arrow exploded in the air before her. It was Bisco's signature King Trumpet, its ivory body stretching toward Pawoo. And in its center, borrowing the ferocious momentum of its growth, came Bisco himself, hurtling like an arrow.

"What?!" Pawoo cried. "You predicted my move?!"

"Everyone seems to have some sort of secret technique," Bisco grumbled. "It's time for me to come up with one, too!"

Having committed fully to her attack, Pawoo was unable to block in time. The world seemed to move in slow motion as Bisco cracked a smile and thrust a mushroom arrow into the tip of his own boot.

"Biscooo!!"

"Now!!"

Boom!

As Pawoo sliced the air with her staff, Bisco leaped atop the weapon, avoiding the follow-up swing by somersaulting through the air. The momentum of his forward flip guided his foot toward Pawoo's exposed back.

"Secret technique!" he yelled. *"Clamshell Heel Drop!!"*

Gaboom!

A mushroom erupted from his boot, flinging his heel down. It amplified the terrifying speed of Bisco's kick, resulting in a move whose sheer destructive capability was immeasurable.

"Ghh…ahhh!"

Pawoo felt her entire body crack underneath its weight. Her rapidly retreating consciousness was able to assemble one last thought before oblivion gripped her.

It…it's beautiful…

Even the pain became pleasure, and as her body shook in perverse enjoyment, she looked up into Bisco's flashing eyes.

No… It's not over yet!!

Pawoo called upon the last of the demon within. She shook her head, using her sleek black hair as a whip to entangle Bisco's foot.

"Wh-whoa?!"

Ker-rash!!

The two fighters slammed into the ground simultaneously, and a cloud of dust blanketed them both. Inside, Bisco rolled up onto his feet and wiped the blood from his brow. However, when he looked at his hand, he noticed the light of the rainbowshroom mixed in with the crimson blood, glowing softly as if waiting for the archer's prayers.

…All right.

Bisco nodded and forced his aching body to stand, waiting for the dust to clear.

The *Ultrafaith Arrow* was Jabi's final gift to his son, and Bisco's unflinching determination was the trigger. Once the rainbowshroom spores in his blood sensed his resolve, the rest was simple.

I just have to believe.

Bisco looked straight ahead. There, in the clearing smoke, stood the warrior woman Pawoo, looking as gallant and stern as she had that day when the two of them first met.

"…You made me so happy," she said. "…The next attack will be my last, Bisco… I love you."

His spouse's words had little effect on him. He sniffed, unconcerned, and replied only:

* * *

"…I know."

Pawoo launched herself at Bisco. She was a streak, a single straight line that moved toward her target in slow motion.

"Don't be afraid, Pawoo. This man will show you the way. He'll take you apart and put you back together again!"

Her indigo eyes flashed.

"Bisco will prevail…"

Their souls reflected off each other. Bisco pulled his bow tight.

"I will prevail…"

Prismatic shades of light enwreathed his arrow, and the spores shook with the magnitude of the prayer contained within them.

""It's time to end this!!""

Ka-chew!!

Bisco's arrow sliced Pawoo's suit, but she twisted out of its path in midair. She moved almost entirely on instinct, but those instincts did not fail her. Now she was in striking range. She raised her staff high over her head and swung it down with enough force to split open her husband's head like a ripe watermelon…

But the staff did nothing more than graze Bisco's nose, embedding its tip in the ground at his feet.

"…Haah! Haah! Haah!"

At the very last moment, Pawoo had returned to her senses and purposefully missed her target. The cause was Bisco's arrow, the one that she had just dodged. Afterward, the arrow had changed direction and struck the Rust flower that clung to the back of Pawoo's neck.

But that wasn't all. An arrow directed at the Rust flower was sure to skewer its host's throat as well. And yet Bisco had stopped his arrow's movement at the last second with nothing more than the power of his own faith, spilling only a few drops of Pawoo's crimson blood. It was an extraordinary evolution of Bisco's new technique, considering he had only learned it a few hours ago.

"You were amazing, Pawoo!" he said. "We've won!"

He took her hand, his jade-green eyes glimmering with absolute respect. The darkness tormenting Pawoo was nowhere to be seen, the brainwashing entirely dispelled. Caked in sweat, she slumped to the ground.

"We...won...?"

"Yeah. The *Ultrafaith Arrow* needs utter conviction to work. You gave me that."

"...I...did...?"

"...Or maybe...," said Bisco, scratching his cheek. "Maybe it's fair to say...I just fell in love with you a little."

Bisco was never one to mince words. Pawoo's eyes went wide at his declaration, and she stopped moving. Bisco felt a pressure unlike any before, and broke into a cold sweat, swiftly averting his gaze and muttering something else to change the subject.

"Still, I'm impressed you managed to miss that strike at the end," he said with a cheeky smile. "Even a wifezilla like you must have achin' muscles by now, huh?"

"...*Sob...sob...*"

"Hmm? H-hey..."

"Waaaaah!"

All of a sudden, Pawoo burst out crying. She hung her head, kneeling over the remnants of the Rust flower, her raven hair spilling on the floor.

"I was just kiddin'," said Bisco "Ain't that our running gag? You don't have to... Wagh!"

"Waaaaaah!!"

Pawoo threw her arms around him, pulling him tight. However, there was none of the bone-breaking strength that usually accompanied her hugs. Instead, she just sobbed softly as the tears rolled down her cheeks.

"It made me so happy!" she wailed. "I was so happy to fight you at full strength..."

"P-Pawoo..."

"I'm sorry! I'm so sorry! It's no way for a wife to behave, I know!"

"Calm down! Stop cryin'! It's fine, ain't it? It ain't just me who's allowed to be selfish all the time. S-stop... You're chokin'... Erk..."

"I love you so much!!"

Pawoo tore off her skullcap and tossed it aside, as if putting her past life behind her. She buried her face in his chest and sobbed like a little girl. Bisco, meanwhile, wasn't sure what to do in this situation. He wanted to embrace her back, but he found himself scared of touching his wife's soft skin, so his arms only hovered uselessly in the air.

Pawoo, however, was not shy about tightening her grip, as though making up for her husband's modesty. Soon, her crushing strength was like that of a boa constrictor strangling a bear, and between that, her tears, and the warmth of her body, Bisco could do nothing but try to keep his bones in one piece.

"L-let go! We ain't got time for this!" he croaked.

"No! Hug me back! Let me feel the arms of someone stronger than myself!!"

"I-I'm tellin' you, we ain't got time to... Aaah!"

Through the hole in the wall, in the night outside, Bisco spotted the fluttering of a cloak. Seconds later, dozens of black machines followed after the figure.

"Milo!" he shouted.

"...What are those? Some kind of robot?" asked Pawoo, placing her head atop Bisco's. "Oh, the Mokujin!" Her tears were all but gone, and as she traced the machines' movements with her eyes, she spotted the jet-black metal of their leader.

"Kurokawa!"

"Looks like Milo needs help," said Bisco. "Let's go!"

"...Curse you. Curse you, curse you, curse you. Curse you for making a fool of me in front of my husband!!"

Pawoo's tears were replaced in an instant with a mask of pure rage. She clenched her teeth and dug her fingers into the ground so hard she left marks in the metal flooring. It was enough to drain all the color from Bisco's cheeks.

"I'm going to tear her face from her body! Bisco, get ready!"

"Um…okay…? Hold on. I can handle myself… Whoa!"

Pawoo slung Bisco under one arm and departed, staff in hand, a black streak across the rooftops of Imihama.

☆⚥↻0⚥ **11**

"Get back here, you sneaky little rodent!"

High over Imihama, Kurokawa scanned the city for Milo. The cameras in her glowing red eye quickly picked out his form. He was carrying Tirol as he leaped through the air.

"Let's see you handle this," she said, pointing her megaphone-shaped arm in his direction. "Ready *Director Cannon*."

Kurokawa was preparing to fire, when all of a sudden…

Pchew!!

"…!! Launch *After Effects*!"

…she spotted a golden arrow out of the corner of her eye, and immediately deployed her dimensional defenses, transforming her megaphone arm back into a five-fingered hand. The Rust-Eater arrow shifted to a downward trajectory as it was sucked through Kurokawa's wall, landing with a *Gaboom!!* in the streets below. Kurokawa's attention quickly shifted to the golden mushroom erupting into the night from the point of impact.

"Oh, excellent," she said. "I can't believe I forgot our leading man. This isn't the time to be pointing the cameras at some two-bit panda costar!"

One eye jet-black, the other glowing red, Kurokawa looked out over the townscape. Atop a tall building in the distance were two jade-green sparks, burning bright. Beside them was another figure with fair skin and raven hair, gripping a staff as if to defend that lustrous light.

"Yes, stay right there, Akaboshi. Don't move a centimeter."

Kurokawa chuckled and deployed the dimensional wall ahead of her once more. Then she backed up a little before setting her thrusters to full blast and flying into it.

"Damn, missed again," said Bisco. "What's that black hazy crap all about?"

"She called it '*After Effects*,'" explained Pawoo. "I'm not sure how it works, but it seems to be capable of transferring flying objects somewhere else. It also can't be destroyed, as it lacks a physical form."

"So my arrows can't hit her, huh? Cheeky bastard."

"It should pose no problem for you, though, my love," said Pawoo, placing her hand on Bisco's shoulder and whispering gently into his ear. "Others' strength is your strength. You are a mushroom man who feeds on the life of your foes. The arrow of your faith will conquer this barrier, just as it conquered me."

"Easy for you to say," Bisco shot back. "I can't just fire those things off whenever I feel like it, you know!"

"Look out! Here she comes!"

Pawoo moved in front of Bisco protectively as a jet-black portal appeared before them. Kurokawa stepped out from it, clapping her hands slowly.

"I must say, I was wondering how you managed to free that gorilla from my brainwashing. An arrow of faith, hmm? Veeery interesting."

From somewhere on her person came the whir of a tape deck. Kurokawa placed her hands to her temples, as though watching something play out in the cinema of her mind.

"The *Ultrafaith Arrow*. Everyone had dismissed it as the mere ramblings of a senile old man. A sharpened will that causes the Rust and spores in the air to react, guiding any projectile to its destination."

"..."

"A technique perfected across two generations of master and student... I knew it. No script could ever contain you, Akaboshi. The only way to portray you is by capturing your truth directly on film."

"Give it up," said Pawoo. "Do you really insist on continuing this farcical production?"

"Of course I do," Kurokawa said, grinning and tapping her glowing red eye. "The camera's still rolling, isn't it? All I need to finish production is right here inside the Perfect Tetsujin. Ah, this was more than worth throwing away my human body…"

"You bastard! Just how far are you willing to go?"

"Let's find out, Akaboshi… It's time for the final showdown. You've traveled all across the land, rescuing your friends, and now it's time to face the one responsible! Will your new arrow be enough to defeat me?!"

Pawoo's eyes burned with rage as she stared Kurokawa down, but for whatever reason, Bisco couldn't seem to muster up the same fury. He lowered his bow and scratched his cheek.

"I…can't be mad at you."

"…What?!"

"Bisco?!" cried Pawoo, turning and yelling at him. "What do you mean, you can't be mad? This woman had you running all over Japan for some measly movie! Her reasons are absurd! She's a psychopath! A villain of the highest order!!"

"You're right, her reasons *are* absurd. To us, at least."

Even Kurokawa could scarcely believe the words coming out of Bisco's mouth. She simply stood and stared blankly.

"'Course, I only realized it after comin' this far, but Kurokawa's serious. This isn't some selfish trick like the shit she pulled when she was a man. She really does want to make the greatest film ever."

"…Rgh…"

Kurokawa's face gradually reddened.

"Actors…are not…allowed…to psychoanalyze the director, Akaboshiii!"

"I don't know what god you worship, but I see the strength of your belief. Now all we gotta do is find out whose faith is stronger."

Bisco looked up. His eyes were as clear as a pool of the purest water.

"…And that's a sacred ritual," he said. "It ain't somethin' you do in anger."

"But then the movie won't make SENSE!" yelled Kurokawa, stamping her feet and destroying the roof they were standing on. Bisco and Pawoo kicked off the rubble and made their way to the neighboring building.

"I'll take her on," said Bisco. "You stand back and watch."

"Right, I'll…," Pawoo began. "…Whaaat?! Are you insane?!"

"I gotta show the proper respect," Bisco explained. "If she wants to make this film so bad, then I think we should let her."

Pawoo stood in shock as Bisco took her staff and gave it a few powerful swings. A moment later, Kurokawa landed on the rooftop, cracking the concrete, her face still red.

"Akaboshi," she said. "Why? Why is it that after all I've done, you still won't hate me?! Why won't you strike me down with righteous fury?! You're a hero! You're supposed to destroy evil, not respect it!"

"Listen up, Kurokawa. If there's one thing I know…" Bisco's sullen demeanor bore a stark contrast to Kurokawa's sheer rage. "…it's that there ain't no such thing as heroes or villains in this world!"

"Urgggh!"

The purehearted light in Bisco's eyes was like a laser beam, piercing Kurokawa's chest.

"The only ones here are me and you! There ain't nothin' 'authentic' about castin' us into your prepared roles!"

Bisco's words were like a slap to the face. Kurokawa could only tremble in embarrassment as Bisco went on.

"I've met a lot of people on this journey," he said. "But none of 'em were evil. They lived and died by their beliefs, just like I'll live and die by mine. We're all just worshipin' our own gods; there ain't no right or wrong in that. So I ain't your hero, Kurokawa, and none of them are villains, even you! If you're serious about capturin' the truth on film, then you gotta stand and give it all you got. But if you're dead set on dyin' the villain, then I'll play along, but there ain't no truth in that."

"Grrrh!!"

Pawoo could hardly contain her disbelief. "Wh-what?!"

"If you're not even gonna try, then neither am I. This staff is all I need to beat you."

"Akaboshi…" Kurokawa finally squeezed out the words. "Despite what you say, you *are* a hero. You're noble and pure, wild and free! I have only one duty, and that is to die by your hand!"

"Drop the bullshit, you third-rate director!!"

Held tight in Bisco's grip, Pawoo's staff carved through the air, striking Kurokawa as she threw up her metallic arm to defend. The director threw out a punch with her other arm, but Bisco evaded it while delivering an overhead swing that caught her in the shoulder.

"I don't give a shit about your reasons," he said, "but if you want me to take you seriously, then you gotta do the same! You got two seconds to decide. Is this film worth fightin' for, or are you just playin' the part?!"

"Aaakaaaboooshiii!!"

Kurokawa twisted. A flash of thigh was all that preceded a roundhouse kick that collided with Bisco's own. The skin cracked along the length of her slender leg.

"Hah! Guess you decided to give it a go after all. You're only a second-rate director now!"

"Launch *Clapper Board Scissor!*"

At Kurokawa's command, her left arm transformed into a clapper board—the kind used at the start of filming to begin a take. With its signature *Clack!* she closed its teeth around Bisco's staff, trapping it.

"You're right…you're right," she said. "I'm still too weak. Too weak to capture the ultimate you!"

The staff groaned within the jaws of Kurokawa's weapon, before finally breaking under its viselike grip. Bisco let out a surprised "Whoa" as Kurokawa swung down with her other arm. But just at that moment, Pawoo jumped in and carried him out of the way.

"Pawoo!" he yelled. "I said to leave us to it, didn't I?"

"Don't be selfish!" she shouted back. "I'll distract her; you find some way to use the *Ultrafaith Arrow!*"

"But she just snapped your staff like a twig. You ain't got a weapon no more!"

"Ha. A mere tool. A true warrior isn't so picky!"

Pawoo strode over to a nearby pile of rubble left from the collapsed roof and, in a fearsome display of strength, wrenched free a length of rebar, giving it a threatening swing.

"I think not, gorilla!" shouted Kurokawa. "Your time in the spotlight is over! Any more of you, and the filmgoers will all flee in terror!"

"Hmph! If you want me to exit stage left, then you'll have to make me!"

Pawoo took up a combat stance, while behind her, Bisco drew his bow.

"Heh, now it finally feels like we're doin' stuff as a couple!"

"Agreed. It's time to cut the cake at last!"

"Aaargh!" howled Kurokawa. "You're messing up the script with your hopeless ad-libbing!"

Pawoo launched herself at her foe, her raven hair streaking behind her like a comet's tail. Her improvised staff made a ringing sound as it struck the Perfect Tetsujin's metallic body.

"Aiieee!! Look out! Right! Right!"

"I know, already! Calm down, Tirol! ...H-hey! Did you just blow your nose on my cloak?!"

Milo carried Tirol on his back, leaping through the Imihama night-scape as he fought off Kurokawa's army of Perfect Mokujin. They were unshakable, dogged in their pursuit even after many of them had been partially destroyed by Milo's mushroom arrows.

After downing one with an anchorshroom, Milo looked out over the rooftops, to the sparks flying from Bisco's battle in the distance.

"It's begun," he said. "We need to hurry. I have to be by Bisco's side, or else...!!"

"Behind us!! Panda, behind us!!"

"Hrh!"

Milo produced his dagger and, in one swift movement, wheeled

around while swinging it at his foe. The blade caught the back of the
Mokujin's neck, severing a clump of cables and detaching the head
from its body.

"Y-yes!" cried Tirol. "You did it!"

"It's no use," lamented Milo. "There's no end to them!"

He landed in a children's playground, surrounded by a fence. However, the thirty or so Mokujin encircled the park, their mechanical
minds linked to one another. Even the one Milo had just felled was
there, the severed cables flailing from its neck like a Hydra's head. The
chances of bringing the fight to a swift conclusion seemed to grow
slimmer by the second.

"If only Bisco were here…," Milo muttered, then quickly shook his
head. "No, I can't always rely on him. I have to do this alone! I have
to…!"

"Milo! Watch out! They're coming!"

"!"

The Mokujin all lunged at once toward the gravel where Milo was
standing. Taking his dagger in one hand, Milo began to chant.

"*Won/shad*— Huh?"

Just then, a shadow passed overhead, blocking out the moonlight.

"Hyo-ho-ho! Squash 'em flat, Actagawa!!"

Ka-boom!!

An enormous orange claw pounded the ground in front of Milo,
flinging sand from the sandbox into the air. The giant crab tore one
of the approaching Mokujin limb from limb, reducing it to scrap in a
matter of seconds.

"*Cough! Cough!* Wh-what happened?!" screamed Tirol.

"…Ahhh!!"

As the dust cleared and the moon shone down on Actagawa's orange
carapace, Milo saw who it was seated in the saddle.

"Kept you waiting, did I?" the rider said with a grin, adjusting the
tricorne hat atop his head. "Well, no matter."

"Jabi!"

"Jabi! …Huh? But…wait… Huh?"

Tirol's face went from joy to confusion to fear in the span of a few seconds.

"Are you…are you a ghost? I mean, ya died, didn't ya? Akaboshi shot ya with his arrow, and then…"

"…He died," said Milo. "Jabi's dead."

"Now's not the time for your jokes, Panda!!"

"Hyo-ho-ho. The kid ain't jokin'. See fer yerself."

Jabi lifted his chin and showed Tirol his throat. To her shock, there was a steel arrowhead plainly visible at the front, its shaft leading back through his neck and through the Rust flower at his nape.

Tirol's mouth flapped wordlessly. Milo spoke calmly, but his voice was filled with sorrow.

"Jabi is dead, biologically speaking. His heart has stopped. But back then…"

"…Bisco's arrow altered my path," finished Jabi. "Took me off the road to death."

He let out one of his signature laughs before taking up Actagawa's reins once more.

"Talk about beatin' a dead horse," he said. "Looks like I got some work to do before I go beddy-bye. Well, suits me fine. At least I get one last swan song before these old bones conk out for good. Go to him, boy. I'll take care of things round here."

"Jabi! We'll beat Kurokawa, just you wait! Then we can…!!"

"Wossat? Musta got some wax in my ears. Can't hear whatever sap you're spoutin'. Can you, Actagawa?"

The giant crab raised his claw against the line of Mokujin in the park and emitted a single bubble in response.

"Ogai coulda swept this lot in five minutes flat back in his heyday," said Jabi, leaning forward in the saddle and whispering to Actagawa. "Wonder if you can measure up to him?"

Actagawa was clearly incensed by this remark. His six legs pounded like bullets, striking the earth and launching him high into the air.

Ker-rash!!

He landed on an Immie-shaped slide, squashing it flat. The two Mokujin standing atop it were pulverized instantly.

"Jabi!" yelled Milo.

"Milo, come back!" said Tirol, grabbing him by the neck and pulling. "You understand what Jabi's doin', don't ya? He's givin' away his precious daughter on his deathbed! And what's a husband-to-be gotta do at a time like this?"

Milo realized at once. "I've got to go to my bride!"

"...I know I said it first," muttered Tirol with a sarcastic look, "but ya didn't have to latch on so quickly!"

Milo kicked off the ground and ascended into the night. As his cloak flapped in the wind, he nocked a mushroom arrow and aimed it at a tall building. The Mokujin attempted to prevent his escape, but Jabi's swift arrows put any would-be interceptors to rest.

"Hold on tight, Tirol!" Milo shouted to the girl on his back. "It's going to be a rough ride!"

"Ain't it always?"

Pchew! Gaboom!!

Milo's King Trumpet shot out of the building at an acute angle, catapulting the two high into the air above Imihama and over toward Bisco's fight.

"Hi-yah!!"

Swoosh! Clang!

Pawoo's magnificent swing only served to make Kurokawa even more irritated.

"How many times do I have to tell you?" she growled. "Your part in this is over!"

Then, with the staff still embedded in her shoulder, Kurokawa countered with her *Clapper Board Scissor*, delivering a sideways sweep that struck Pawoo hard in the stomach and sent her crashing to the floor.

"Leave the scene," she said, steam rising from her ears. "You are relieved of your role!"

She then raised her *Director Cannon*, but as she prepared to fire, she heard the *Twang!!* of Bisco's bow and let out a startled gasp.

"*After Effects!!*" she cried, and Bisco's solar arrow disappeared into the four-dimensional vortex that emanated from her arm. It reappeared behind her and sunk into the earth, whereupon the blossoming mushroom flung her forward with a *Gaboom!*.

"Pawoo!" Bisco cried.

"I'm okay!" Pawoo shouted back between blood-filled coughs. "This is nothing. Are you able to fire the *Ultrafaith Arrow* yet?"

"Hmm...," said Bisco, scratching the back of his head. "I dunno. I just ain't got the motivation. It only comes when I gotta save Milo, rescue you, shit like that."

Suddenly, there was a loud bang as Kurokawa blew the mushroom away with her arm cannon. She stepped out of the smoke, half human, half cyborg, her whole face flushed red with anger and embarrassment.

"So what you're saying," she growled, "is that I'm still not strong enough for you to go all out?!"

"That ain't what I'm sayin'! It's just..."

"Yes, it is!!"

Bisco scooped up Pawoo and leaped to the side, moments before the blast from Kurokawa's cannon obliterated the spot they'd been standing. Rolling to his feet, Bisco turned to bark something back—but when he saw Kurokawa, he froze in shock.

"...*Sob...sob...*"

She was crying. On the side that still bore Mepaosha's face, large tears dribbled down her cheek and onto her exposed chest.

"It's true, I'm not fit to play this role. You know, after I died, I looked back on my life, and decided I had to live more authentically... That's why I threw it all away: my shame, my respect for society... I threw it all away so I could bare myself to you! You don't know what I've had to sink to in order to get where I am today, Akaboshi, to have you here on my set...and it's still not enough! Even this stupid machine body isn't enough! What do I have to do to make you take me seriously?!"

* * *

Neither Bisco nor Pawoo could believe what they were seeing. That woman, that incarnation of evil, was sobbing like a child. A look of utter despair on her face, she pointed her *Director Cannon* upward, and right before their eyes, it expanded into the form of a large parabolic antenna.

"*Director Cannon: Armageddon.*"

"Wh-what?! What are you doing?!" cried Bisco.

"*Sob.* In...in just one minute, this attack will scatter nuclear bombs all across the country. I—I may not be able to defeat you, Akaboshi, but at least I can leave this land a scorched earth in my wake."

As she cried, Kurokawa gathered the Rust particles in her arm. The jet-black cannon glowed with rapidly increasing brightness and emitted a rumbling groan that shook the very air.

"Is this...still not enough, Akaboshi? Is this still not enough to make you care?!"

"Get a grip! How old are you?!"

The Rust-Eater spores within Bisco flared up, and he loosed arrow after arrow toward his foe, but Kurokawa's dimensional barriers were now fully automatic, and they deflected the projectiles in all directions. Even Bisco was feeling the pressure now, and tiny beads of sweat formed across his brow.

"I-it's no use," he said. "I can't use the *Ultrafaith Arrow!*"

"Bisco, do something! Kurokawa's about to destroy the whole country!"

"I know! I know! But so what?! I don't give a crap what happens to Japan! All this theory and posturin' is givin' me a headache! It doesn't make me *feel* anything."

"Aaargh! Dammit! Dammit!!"

Bisco's words only seemed to enrage Kurokawa further. Now she was crying streams of tears, and the weapon she held aloft steadily grew in power.

"So be it!" she yelled. "The last shot of the film will be a wide-angle cut of death and destruction! Three, two..."

Beyond the reach of bow and staff, Kurokawa was nothing but a ticking time bomb, ready to explode. Pawoo threw herself across her husband in a last-ditch effort to save his life.

But at that moment, there was a flash of crimson, and a whip wrapped itself around Kurokawa's right shoulder.

"One! …Huh?"

"It's time to put a stop to this two-bit production of yours, you fool!"

Crkcrkcrkcrkcrk!!

A red spark traveled along the length of the whip, preventing Kurokawa's cannon from firing. Then the spark ran through her body, disabling her defense systems.

"Wh-whoaaa?! Wh-what's happening?!"

"There's no point in struggling," came a voice. "My Ox-Head Whip has the ability to disrupt the Perfect Tetsujin program!!"

Behind Kurokawa, before Bisco's and Pawoo's stunned eyes, stood a woman, her red dress and blond hair fluttering in the backlash of her whip and her forehead glimmering with sweat.

"I've waited a looong time for this, Mepaosha," she said, an unsettling sneer on her face. "You weren't the only one who partnered with Matoba Heavy Industries, remember!"

"Wh-who's she…?!"

"Gopis!!"

"Akaboshi! I can't hold her for long!"

Bisco looked on in shock, and Kurokawa glared bitterly as Gopis barked her instructions. The ring piercing in her nose chimed with every word.

"While she's trapped in the Ox-Head Whip, she can't use *After Effects*! Shoot her in the head or the heart or wherever while you still can!"

"O-of all people…!" Kurokawa murmured with hellish vindictiveness. "Of all people, how could *you* defy me?! You're not an actor! You're not even a staff member or an extra! You're just a pebble by the side of the road! A cow caked in human makeup!"

"Keh-heh-heh. Oh, long have I waited to see that foolish face of yours. How humiliating is it to be outwitted by some blond bimbo? Besides, you wear just as much makeup as me."

"Diiiieeee!!"

Even while paralyzed, Kurokawa focused her power into her robotic limbs, swinging her *Clapper Board Scissor* down on Gopis's head. However, just before the attack connected, Pawoo leaped in and sent it flying aside with her staff.

"Bisco! Now!" she yelled.

Hearing this, Kurokawa turned to where Bisco stood, bow drawn, the light of the Rust-Eater illuminating his entire body.

"Akaboshi…"

"You've done enough, Kurokawa." He grinned, flashing his canines. "We'll continue this in hell! I got a few casting recommendations you can scout while you're down there!"

"Akaboshiiiii!! I'm not done!!"

Shuf!

Bisco loosed his golden arrow, and it landed right in Kurokawa's chest. She staggered, and then a second arrow hit her, and a third. The momentum of each strike caused her body to fly this way and that, and then…

Gaboom! Gaboom! Gabooom!!

…an explosion of Rust-Eaters scattered her mechanical parts across the roof. Half-eaten by the mushrooms, Kurokawa could do nothing but emit a wordless groan. She fell to her knees, a vast quantity of steam rising off her… And then she stopped moving completely.

"Phew! Yes… We did it!" cried Gopis. "Ha…! She's dead! Ha-haa! You're dead, you idiot!!"

"Calm yourself," scolded Pawoo, catching the blond-haired woman as she, too, fell to the roof. "So you're Gopis, vice-warden of Six Realms? What are you doing here?"

"Cleaning up her mess," Gopis answered between ragged breaths. "A-after all, it was 'cause of me that Kurokawa came back in the first place…"

Bisco came over, too, and peered down at her.

"We both signed up at Six Realms at the same time," she went on. "We needed the power of the Benibishi to complete production on the Perfect Tetsujin. B-but she undid Matoba's safety protections and made modifications to herself while I wasn't looking..."

"So you were acting on behalf of Matoba?" asked Pawoo.

"Ha! I couldn't give less of a shit about that company. I just always wanted to get back at her. She can do whatever she wants with her body, but I've never forgiven her for making *me* get a sex change, too...! *Cough! Cough!*"

Pawoo tried to make Gopis comfortable, while Bisco turned and walked over to the kneeling body of Kurokawa, now riddled with mushrooms.

"...

　"...

　"...

"...Ugh..."

A single groan escaped her lips.

"Akaboshi... Do you think I was...boring?"

Bisco didn't answer. He just stared straight at her with his jade-green eyes.

"I didn't die that day at your hand, Akaboshi. I was reborn! Your arrow released me from a prison of lies and platitudes, bared my soul for all to see! ...You're a hero, Akaboshi! *My* hero!"

A few moments of silence, and then:

"You are my star, Akaboshi. My Antares. I wanted to gaze at you, see how long you could twinkle in my sky. That's all I ever wanted..."

Kurokawa paused to retch up a number of Rust-Eater stalks. As she did, her signature sunglasses fell from her nose and onto the floor.

"I don't want to die... Not without seeing your ultimate technique. Please... I have to see—"

Slap!!
Bisco struck Kurokawa hard across the cheek. Then, when she placed her hand to the mark and stared back at him in shock, he headbutted her in the face.

"Then why don't you get off your ass and quit whinin' about it?!" he yelled.

Even Gopis and Pawoo were stunned by Bisco's words. All eyes turned to him.

"If you take my arms, I'll bite you to death. If you break my teeth, I'll stare you to death. *That's* what true determination is about. If you're ready to curl up and die after just a few mushrooms, how the hell do you think you're gonna unleash my full potential?!"

"...Who could possibly survive that?" muttered Pawoo. But before her very eyes, the utterly defeated Kurokawa slowly rose to her feet once more.

"I-if I have no arms, I'll bite you to death..."

"Yes! That's the spirit! Now stand, Kurokawa!"

"'Whaaat?!'" Gopis and Pawoo screamed in unison.

"You say I'm your star. Then throw everything away and reach for it!"

"If you break my teeth...I'll stare you to death...!"

Kurokawa reached out and snatched Bisco's offered hand, looking up into his eyes.

At that moment, the wind whipped up around them, and Bisco's hair flared prismatic. A gust swept up the rainbowshroom spores, forming an aurora in the skies above Imihama.

"Huh? What's happening?" said Bisco.

"Akaboshiii!"

The rainbowshroom spores, harbingers of the *Ultrafaith Arrow*... This time, Bisco wasn't the one to summon them. It was Kurokawa's prayers that resonated within him, awakening the spores of possibility.

Bisco understood that, so he quietly pulled an arrow from his quiver. As he did so, a rainbow light spread from his fingers across the shaft, turning the arrow a multitude of different colors.

"Y-yes, that's right, Bisco! Finish her off!"

"Yeah! This fool has hung on long enough!"

Bisco glanced back at Pawoo and Gopis, then turned to face Kuro-kawa once more.

"...Seems like your prayers gave birth to this arrow, Kurokawa."

"A...ka...bo...shi..."

"It's time for take two. Show me the strength of your faith!"

Bisco leveled his bow and fired. At point-blank range, the arrow pierced Kurokawa's heart, its rainbow shaft plunging deep within her breast.

...And then the light began to spread across her body.

"Yes!" cheered Gopis. "At last, that fool Mepaosha is—"

"Wait," interrupted Pawoo. "Something's not right."

Pawoo watched as the Rust-Eater mushrooms across Kurokawa's body were sucked back into her. Glowing in all the colors of the rainbow, she steadily rose to her feet.

"...Akaboshi."

Her pine-needle hair now shimmered in seven colors, as if all the evil had been purged from her body.

"Am I finally ready?" asked Kurokawa. "Ready to be your foe, your rival...?"

Bisco nodded wordlessly and smiled. He looked across at Kurokawa, wrapped in the glow of the aurora. She was smiling, too. She leaped off in the direction of the prefectural bureau, carving a rainbow trail in the sky as she went.

"B-Bisco?! What did you do to her?!"

"Well," he answered, sheepishly scratching his cheek. "When I shot her with the *Ultrafaith Arrow*, I guess she kinda took that power into herself."

"W-wait, so K-Kurokawa has the p-power of the rainbowshroom?!" said Gopis, collapsing weakly to her knees.

"A-are you insane?!" said Pawoo, grabbing Bisco by the shoulders and shaking him violently. "Do you have any idea what you've just done?! That woman is a cocktail of death and destruction!!"

"Yeah, but she's not *evil*... Okay, maybe she's a little bit evil, but... what's the word? She's purehearted. I just wanted to talk to her some more..."

"Y-you simpleton!!" Pawoo cried, wringing Bisco's neck.

Just then, from atop the building where Kurokawa stood, a single beam of multicolored light shot up into the sky. Passing through the atmosphere and into space, the beam tore through a satellite orbiting near the moon. The resulting explosion lit up the city of Imihama like midday.

"Whoa, now we're talkin'."

"You've unleashed a god of destruction," said Pawoo. "Are you sure you can beat it?"

"'Course I can," Bisco retorted. His cloak and hair fluttered rainbow-colored in the breeze. "Against a foe like that, firin' the *Ultrafaith Arrow* is as easy as pie!"

Bisco launched himself into the air with a sonic boom, leaving tiny rainbowshrooms where he had just been standing. Pawoo watched his glimmering trail recede into the sky.

"...What a hopeless man... But I suppose that's why I love you."

She sighed, then noticed Gopis laid out on the floor, frothing at the mouth. She quickly rushed over to give the woman a helping hand.

"Wh-what's that?!"

The townsfolk of Imihama gazed up in fear and wonder at the prefectural bureau. Atop that towering building, colorful beams of light shot out in all directions, raining down destruction on far-off mountains and even neighboring prefectures.

"I-is that...Kurokawa?!" yelled Milo, stopping at the corner of a rooftop and staring dumbfounded at the sight before him. "What's going on?!"

He watched as a second figure was swatted away from the building, falling through the night sky like a multicolored shooting star.

"That's Bisco!!" he shouted, and with lightning-fast reflexes, he hopped over to catch him, barely making it before the figure hit the ground.

Ker-rash!!

"Oww...," groaned Milo, knocked flat by the impact. "...Bisco! Are you okay?!"

"Damn. She's way stronger than I thought...," muttered Bisco in response, wiping the blood from his nose. "The *Ultrafaith Arrow* ain't workin'. I can't hit her."

"What?! The *Ultrafaith Arrow* missed her?! That's impossible!"

"See for yourself."

Bisco tore off his cat-eye goggles and fixed them to Milo's head. Turning up the magnification, Milo could make out the rainbow form of Kurokawa standing atop the prefectural building. Around her, like a buzzing fly, was Bisco's arrow. Each time it tried to pierce her, it disappeared into a dimensional shroud that cloaked her entire body, reappearing out the other side without ever once touching her.

"What the...?! She's covered herself in *After Effects*!"

"My prayers and her prayers are equal. We ain't never gonna win like this."

"...Bisco! Watch out!"

Milo swept his emerald cube in an arc as one of the rainbow beams came hurtling toward them. Immediately, a green mantra barrier appeared around the boys. The beam crashed into it, scattering rainbowshroom spores everywhere, like fireworks.

"It's taking all my effort just to defend!" Milo said. "Bisco, you have to take the shot!"

"I know! But..."

Bisco took up his bow, but as Kurokawa had nullified the *Ultrafaith Arrow*'s effects once already, he found it impossible to muster up the conviction required to fire.

"Dammit, I just need one more shot!"

Bisco looked to his partner, who was sweating with the strain of deflecting the rainbow beams, when suddenly, they heard a voice.

"Listen up, y'all! I'm jackin' the airwaves to bring everyone this special broadcast, live from Imihama! Feast yer eyes on this!"

""Tirol!!""

The boys turned to see the jellyfish girl alongside an army of Immies, pointing an enormous film camera their way.

"They've saved ya from monks, cities, and giant islands!" she yelled into her head-mounted microphone. *"Now Bisco and Milo need your support! If all y'all have any words of gratitude, let's hear 'em!"*

✳ ✳ ✳

"Nuts! Get over here quick! Bisco's on TV!"

"Milo's about to lose… I believe in you! You can do it!"

"Get up, Akaboshi! I'm not lettin' you die here!"

"H-hold on, Nuts! Stop shaking the set!"

"All of you, get on your knees and pray! We ain't stoppin' till Akaboshi's home safe!!"

""""Y-yes, sir!!!"""""

✳ ✳ ✳

"Haaah!!"

"Priest Kandori, sir, please settle down! You're liable to pop a vessel!"

"So what if I do? Lord Akaboshi, our founder, is in trouble! We of the Wizened must prepare our strongest prayers at once! Are you with me, men?!"

""""Yes, sir!!"""""

"Won-culvero-akabosha!"

""""*Won-culvero-akabosha!*"""""

"Won-culvero-akaboshaaa!!"

✳ ✳ ✳

"Vwoo."

"Wh-whaah?! I-it's you! *Cough!* The Akaboshi Mark I! You've come back!"

"Vwoo."

"The TV? *Cough!* Ohh, I see. Akaboshi and Nekoyanagi seem to be in real trouble this time, don't they?"

"...*Vwoo...*"

"What is that? Are you...praying? How could a Mokujin like you possibly—?"

"*VWOOO!!*"

"All right, all right! I'll do it, too. *Cough!* I never thought a man of science like myself would be beseeching a god for help..."

* * *

"*Ouya!*"

"""*Ouya!*"""

"*Ouya!*"

"""*Ouya!*"""

"*Ouya!*"

"""*Ouya!*"""

"E-Elder...I beg of you...let us rest..."

"*Ouya!*"

"""*Ouya!*"""

* * *

"Well, look at that, darling. Don't I know that face?"

"Who is it, your ex? I've told you to stop thinking about him. He's married now, you know."

"No! Look! On the TV! Isn't that the man we met doing initiations for the Gilded Elephants? You know, the one we branded?"

"Why, isn't it just?! Ravishing as ever, isn't he? Ooh, and the boy beside him isn't half-bad, either!"

"So what's going on? Is this a film? If I didn't know better, I'd say our boy's on the tail end of a whipping."

"When did he become an actor? He must be playing the villain; he certainly has the face for it."

"Oh, wouldn't it be hilarious if he won?"

"I'll say."

"Let's cheer him on. Come on, gorgeous!"

""Knock them silly, bad boy!""

* * *

"Mr. Inoshige! C-come in and look at this!!"

"Snakes alive?! It's 'im! Akaboshi!!"

"Nekoyanagi's with him, too, Mr. Inoshige! They're in Imihama!"

"Musta gotten on the wrong side of Kurokawa, the poor git! Give her what for, Akaboshi! Pay that bastard back for all the hippos she slaughtered after takin' over Gunma!"

"Let's cheer him on, Mr. Inoshige! Come on!"

* * *

""""Come on, Akaboshi!! You can do it!!"""""

There was a sound like thunder, and all of a sudden, the heavens parted, and from the clouds descended a flurry of mysterious spores.

"Wh-whoaaa?!"

The spores encircled Bisco, becoming one with his rainbow shroud. The light returned to his jade-green eyes, which shone brighter than ever before.

"Bisco! Are you okay?"

"…I can shoot again! I dunno how, but the rainbowshroom spores have reawakened!"

Bisco exhaled a multicolored breath and drew his bow taut.

"Here I go! Three, two…"

"Not so fast, my boy!"

An orange meteor fell out of the sky and landed next to Bisco, protecting the boys from the laser light just as Milo's barrier was about to shatter.

"Jabi! Actagawa!" he shouted.

"You're missin' somethin'," Jabi said. "Right now, you can only *kill* Kurokawa; if you wanna *save* her, you'll need the most important prayer of all!" He smiled in the multicolored light. "Leave these beams to me," he said. "I should be able to hold 'em for ten seconds!"

"The most important…prayer…?" Bisco repeated uncertainly.

"Bisco!!"

Milo appeared beside him, his hands wrapped around Bisco's bow and arrow. Now free to cast his magic, Milo used his cube to transform the weapon into the Mantra Bow.

"Were you really planning to fire without me?" he asked.

"M-Milo?!"

"I'll have to remind you why I'm here, Bisco. Look at me, and don't look away!"

Bisco met Milo's eyes head-on. They were sapphires of burning flame. Dazzling, blinding. A mysterious current ran through Bisco's body, shocking his skin and electrifying his hair. The rainbowshroom spores were out of control, spilling out of his body, wrapping Milo, the bow, Jabi, and even Actagawa in the same aurora of light.

"I believe in you," Milo said. "Even the whole world's prayers don't hold a candle to mine!"

Milo smiled, his hair now the same rainbow color as Bisco's own. Bisco grinned back, flashing his canines, and together the two boys drew their singular bow against Kurokawa, far off in the distance.

"Let's go! It's time to call it a wrap, Bisco!"

"Finishing move!"

""*Ultrafaith Arrow, Second Order!!*""

It was no arrow but a streak of rainbow light that left the pair's bow. Just as Actagawa's shell was beginning to crack, that light bore the brunt of Kurokawa's beams and tore through them to reach its target.

"*!!*"

Kurokawa spotted the approaching rainbow and immediately redirected her lasers for defense.

"Oh, it's beautiful, Akaboshi. But can it pierce my—?"

Ker-thunk!

"?!"

Kurokawa watched in horror as the rainbow arrow stuck straight into the dimensional barrier, as though it were as solid as any wall. Even more terrifying, it seemed to still be moving, cracking her defense apart, dead set on reaching Kurokawa's stomach.

"An arrow that can pierce higher dimensions...?!"

Crk! Crk! Crk!

"S-so that's how far you've come, Akaboshi... That's how strong your faith is..."

Nothing was safe from this omnipresent arrow of sheer divine power. Kurokawa channeled all her strength Into maintaining the barrier's integrity, but its collapse was inevitable.

Kurokawa had already been shot. And she knew it.

"Kh...kah-ha-ha! Ha-ha-ha! I did it! I finally did it!"

She laughed!

"I got it on film! Your miracle! The true Akaboshi!!"

"Hey! Kurokawa!"

From the other side of her dimensional barrier, she heard Bisco's clear voice ring out in the night.

"That there is mine and Milo's true strength! Did you get it?!"

"A-Akaboshi!!" Kurokawa shouted, her pine-needle hair flapping in the wind. *"I did! A perfect final scene! The light of Antares, obliterating the sad ending I'd written for you!!"*

"I ain't lookin' for a gig fee. Just promise me one thing!"

Bisco, supported by Milo, gazed up at Kurokawa, where she stood on the brink of defeat and destruction. With a flash of his canines... he smiled.

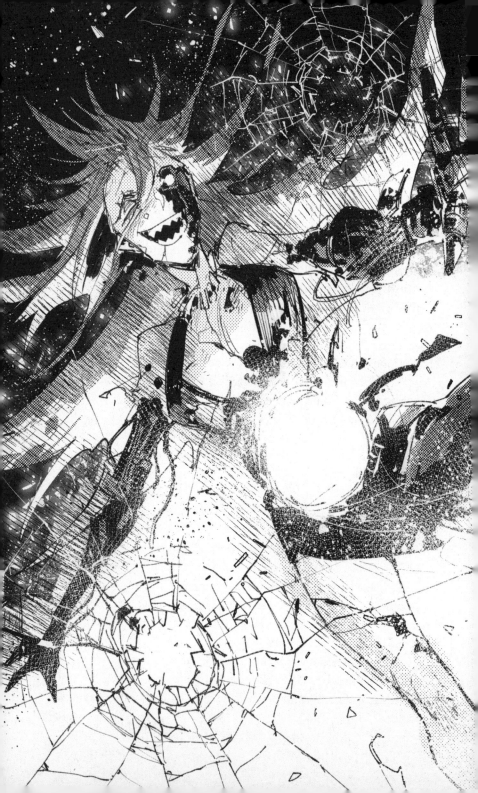

"Promise me when we next meet, you'll drop the act, Kurokawa!"

"Akaboshi!! I… I…!
"I'm so glad I…!"

Ka-shoom!
The rainbow arrow shattered Kurokawa's dimensional wall to pieces and, as if by fate, pierced her stomach—the very place the boys had shot her all those years before.
"Aaaaaah!!"
The arrow carried Kurokawa up and up, through the clouds and high above the stratosphere. The rainbowshroom spores scattering from her body left an aurora trail in the sky, so high up that everyone in the country could see it.

"Aaah! My sky, a rainbow sky!"

As Kurokawa's body began to crumble apart, she uttered her final words.

"I love you, Akaboshi. I love you.
  "They'll give me an Oscar for this, for sure!!"

Gaboom!!!
The explosion was felt all across Japan. The *Second-Order Ultrafaith Arrow* reacted with the rainbowshroom spores in Kurokawa's body, scattering thousands upon thousands of mushrooms into the upper atmosphere. The rainbow fungi clumped together and began rising. Up and up into space they rose, leaving Earth's grip entirely and becoming a tiny planet, twinkling in the night sky.

"Wh-what on earth just happened?!" cried Gopis from where she sat, slumped over on the rooftop.
"Hmm…" Pawoo stood, unperturbed, amid the tiny rainbow

particles that fell like snow. "Well, to cut a long story short, it seems Bisco turned Kurokawa into a planet."

"That's too short, you fool!!"

Then something descended softly from the sky, wrapped in rainbow dust. It seemed to drift directly toward Pawoo, so she caught it, eyeing it curiously.

"What's this?" she asked.

"A recording microchip, looks like," said Gopis, suddenly appearing over her shoulder. "From the camera in Kurokawa's brain, if I had to guess. That should have the whole battle from start to finish on it. Best to just crush it and forget about it."

"…"

Pawoo took the chip in her right hand and began to squeeze… Then she stopped and put it away in her pocket instead. She glanced over to a nearby rooftop, where…

""Zzz…""

…she spied four figures: two boys, an old man, and a crab, snoozing away.

"For shame!" she said, frowning. "Do they not know how eagerly we have awaited their safe return?"

Then she smiled and leaped through the rainbow-filled city to be by their side.

᚛ᚁᚔ᚜ **12**

Rust-Eater Becomes Box Office Smash Hit, Raking in Over Two Hundred Million Sols on Opening Weekend!!

Experts suggest Academy Award judges may rethink their choices!

Rust-Eater has been drawing great crowds ever since its release. Helmed by the late Director Kurokawa, former governor of Imihama Prefecture, the project threw all of Japan into chaos. However, there are still some voices disagreeing with the mainstream buzz:

"The late Director Kurokawa said that she placed a heavy emphasis on authenticity, and yet I feel like that promise was betrayed. The second half of the film demanded some fairly strong suspension of disbelief, introducing arrows that went wherever their archers desired, or arrows that entered other dimensions. The CGI was also turned up to eleven (especially on those rainbow effects!), diminishing the overall quality of the film." (Film Festival staff)

"What a waste to use all this new and unexplored technology for a stupid movie." (Ex-developer at a large company)

"Seats too small." (Prefectural Magistrate)

The film continues to sweep the nation. How will history remember this controversial work of art? We at *Imihama News* can no sooner take our eyes off these startling developments than we can the film itself!

Editorial: Back in the Governor's Seat! Pawoo Nekoyanagi's Muscular Manifesto! (page 3)

The comic strip "Li'l Akaboshi" is on hiatus due to the health of the author.

*   *   *

"Ahhh! Look over there! It's the assistant director! Miss Ochagama, face the camera!"

"A few moments of your time, if you please!"

"Huh? Aw, gee, if y'all insist…"

At the Academy Awards Ceremony, a jellyfish-haired girl in a stylish suit stepped out of a white, open-topped sports car, flanked by security. The light of the camera flashes reflected off her sunglasses, and she looked as smugly satisfied as ever.

"But make it quick, ya hear? I'm a busy woman!"

"Assistant Director!" shouted a reporter, holding his microphone out over a security guard's shoulder. "We know that Kurokawa's death resulted in all production rights being transferred to you. But can we ask, how much of the profits are going directly into your pock—?"

"Another one askin' about money. Toss him out."

"W-wait! Waaah!"

Tirol watched as the guard physically threw the reporter from the premises, then stepped out onto the red carpet as if it were in her very own home. As she waved to the crowd, one woman and a couple of children watched over her from a distance.

"I can't tell if she's clever or just plain shameless," said one of the children, a boy in a shark mask, removing his turban snail hat in order to scratch his head. "Almost dyin' countless times and she still manages to turn it to her advantage."

"That's just who Tirol is, Nuts," said Pawoo with a pretty smile, ruffling his hair. The young boy went rosy-cheeked before looking up at her, indignant, and putting the snail shell hat forcibly back on his head.

"If she hadn't been there," Pawoo went on, "I wouldn't be alive. So I can forgive her a little moneymaking, if that's what she wants. Besides, she spends money as quickly as she earns it, that one."

"But have you even seen the movie, Governor?" Nuts asked. "I don't get what the big deal is. I mean, sure, Akaboshi's scenes were all cool and flashy, but most of the film was just Kurokawa talking to herself."

"Yes. Well, I see your point. I didn't make much of it, either," Pawoo replied, casting her gaze into the distance, as though reminiscing about something. "But when I saw it," she said, "I realized something. Kurokawa wasn't evil at all. She was someone who loved Bisco deeply. Differently to how Milo and I do, perhaps, but still love. She wanted to make her own darkness as dark as possible, so that he could shine ever brighter within it."

"But then...why did she make it into a movie?"

Pawoo thought for a moment, then spoke as if to nobody in particular. "...I guess...she wanted something to be proud of. She wanted to show the whole world what the person she loved was like."

Nuts had never seen his boss so sentimental before. He couldn't take his eyes off her as she gazed wistfully into the distance. He considered teasing her for it, but thought better of the idea, lest he receive a karate chop to the nose again.

"Sounds like they're about to announce the awards," said Pawoo. "Shall we watch?"

"Who cares? It already broke the box office," said Nuts. Then he looked around. "Hey, come to think of it, where's Akaboshi and Nekoyanagi? They're the leading actors! Shouldn't they be here?"

"They have something important to do," Pawoo replied. "In fact, Tirol and I wanted to go with them, but we were told it was Mushroom Keepers only."

"Wh-what could be more important than this?!"

"Ladies and gentlemen!!"

Up on the stage, a portly gentleman threw his arms wide in greeting, to rapturous applause.

"It is my great pleasure to welcome you all to the twentieth annual Japan Film Festival, After Armageddon! It makes me especially proud to see all the hardworking talent who pour out their blood, sweat, and tears year after year in an attempt to rebuild our civilization's great filmmaking lega—"

"Just read out the winners already!!"

"Why do you always take so long rambling?!"

The announcer paused, looking disappointed. *"... Then without further ado, let me proceed straight to announcing the recipients of our most esteemed honor."*

An assistant handed him a bright-red envelope. He opened it, smiled, then looked up at the audience and took a deep breath.

Tirol, Pawoo, and Nuts all leaned forward in anticipation...

"The Academy Award this year goes to...!"

* * *

In a Mushroom Keeper village on the island of Shikoku...

A handpicked group of the greatest tribal warriors was assembled at a large tent erected at the center of the settlement, and they were all rubbing their hands in prayer. Everyone was sweating hard from the flaming torches the priests swung, the endless pounding of the drums, and the strong scent of incense that filled the air.

In the center of it all, atop a bed surrounded by torches, lay Jabi, hero of the Mushroom Keepers, breathing heavily with an arrow still lodged in his neck.

"Wheeze...wheeze...wheeze..."

Though the *Ultrafaith Arrow* could stave off premature death, it could not alter Jabi's natural life span. Perched on the edge of oblivion, Jabi was ready to draw his life to a close.

"Jabi! How are you? Can you breathe all right?!"

"Please, let me give you an anesthetic! You don't need to suffer like this!"

Two boys stood next to him, holding his quivering hand. But Jabi was having none of it.

"Shut the hell up! Lemme die in peace! *Wheeze...wheeze...* Me vision's gettin' blurry... Guess it's the end of ol' Akemi Hebikawa..."

""Jabi!!""

Bisco and Milo held on tightly to his hand, tears in their eyes. Then the other Mushroom Keepers, unable to wait any longer, placed their hands on the boys' shoulders and stepped in front.

"Jabi!" one of them said. "You were our pride. May you live on as the Godbow and stand at the right hand of Enbiten himself. Pray, watch over us from heaven."

"Give my wishes to my husband when you get there!"

"My wife is up there as well. Let her know I'm okay, will you?"

"And my old man!"

"And my grandson!"

"Gaaagh! I ain't rememberin' all these! Write me a list or somethin'!"

The ferocity of an old man in his last five minutes of life was so great, the Mushroom Keepers caved and returned to their prayers. With his remaining strength, Jabi hauled himself up and grabbed on tightly to Bisco's hand.

"I…I can't see! Are ya still there, Bisco, my boy?"

"Jabi! I'm here! I'm right here! Are you okay? Can you hear me?"

"Oh, Bisco, I don't wanna go after all!!"

Then, all of a sudden, the two crashed their foreheads together…and smiled through their tears.

"I still wanna beat ya, Bisco!! I wish I could be young again, and fight ya with all I got! There's still so much I wanna do, lad!"

"Get a grip, old man! We all gotta go sometime!"

Bisco hugged his master tight, and all his tears flowed out. But these were not tears of sorrow for his dying father figure, no. They were tears of love—the kind of love that could never be expressed with mere words.

"Is there anythin' I can help you do in the next minute?" he asked. "Anythin' at all, just make it quick!"

"A minute?! Hrm, let me think…"

Jabi turned the pages of his notebook, straining his eyes as hard as he could to read its contents. He flipped to the very end, where he had written…

GO ALL OUT WITH BISCO.

…and ticked off the entry.

"There ain't nothin' left!" he wailed. "I've done everythin' I wanted to do. There's nothin'…"

Then, on the very brink of death, Jabi's eyes flew open.

"Aaah!"

"What is it, Jabi?!"

"Wine!" he said. "There's a wine made from the tongue of the Pipe Snake that only the elder is allowed to drink! There should be some in his hut. One drop, that's all I ask…"

"Got it!" said Bisco, standing up and wiping his eyes. "Just you wait, Jabi! I'll bring it to you right away!!"

"W-wait, Bisco!" cried Milo. "You can't go!"

"Milo, look after Jabi for me!" he said. "Hold his hand as tightly as you can!"

Bisco leaped out of the tent faster than Milo had ever seen him move before. He flew over to the elder's hut, crashing through the wall.

"Where's the wine?" he yelled.

"Eeek!! Demon!!" shrieked the elder's wife, fainting on the spot. Bisco ignored her and sniffed the air, searching the premises like a starving wolf.

"…There!!"

Ker-rash!!

Bisco somersaulted, delivering a kick that split the elder's chair in two. Beneath it lay a locked trapdoor leading to a hidden basement. Bisco smashed in the door before hurrying down the staircase.

"Pipe Snake wine… Pipe Snake wine…!!"

As he suspected, the basement was a wine cellar containing bottles of all shapes and sizes. Finding a single variety out of all these should have been an impossible task—but not to Bisco's trained senses. He strode straight to the back of the room, where a shrine of sorts contained a single bottle with the character for *Pipe* emblazoned artistically across the label.

"Found it!!"

Boom!

"Eek!!"

Bisco shot off like a rocket, once again terrifying the poor elder's wife on his way out. Faster than one of his own arrows, he returned to the tent where Jabi lay.

"Jabi!!" he said, striding in. "I found it for you! The wine! The Pipe Snake wine!!"

However, Bisco arrived to a silent room. Nobody answered his cry.

"Bisco…!"

Only Milo turned to see him as he entered. His face was drenched with tears.

"Jabi's… He's…!"

Milo couldn't finish his sentence. Seeing his partner collapse to the ground, Bisco walked, slowly, to the center of the tent, as crowds of Mushroom Keepers parted to let him through.

"…

"Jabi."

His eyes lay open.

His full, white whiskers, his tight lips, his noble mien. All were as graceful and dignified as a god's.

"…"

Bisco reached out and stroked Jabi's face, closing his eyelids.

"This is good-bye, old man. But not forever. Once you've settled down, I'll be comin' to see you. Jabi… Dad… Thank you."

He closed his eyes and gently placed his forehead to Jabi's. Then he stood, took the open bottle of wine in his hands, and poured a couple drops into his departed master's mouth.

…And after that, he proceeded to down the entire rest of the bottle in a single gulp.

A stir erupted from the crowd, none louder than from Milo. His partner never drank, and the alcohol content of this single bottle was off the charts.

"B-Bisco! What have you done?! You'll…"

"Jabi, Godbow, hero of the Mushroom Keepers, is dead!!" Bisco yelled, his clear voice sending an electric shock down the spines of all those present. The others stood at attention, listening carefully to Bisco's words.

"Our hero has shed his mortal flesh and ascended to heaven, to live forever as Kyuuseiten, the Godbow! On this blessed day, we mark the birth of a new god! Join me in calling out his name!"

The Mushroom Keepers hesitated for only a moment.

"…Jabi!"

""Jabi!!""

""Kyuuseiten, the Godbow!!""

""May Mushroom Keepers thrive under his protection!""

All voices cried out Jabi's name. All hands lifted their bows to the heavens. Bisco turned to Milo and grinned. He wasn't crying anymore. Milo dried the tears from his own eyes and gave the most brilliant smile he could muster.

"All right, everybody, it's time to start things off with a bang! Get ready!"

Following Bisco's lead, the crowd opened their arms wide. The flames burned brighter, and the drums reached a fever pitch.

"Tonight, we drink to Jabi's ascendency!"

""Hurrah!!""

Clap!

AFTERWORD

"You've grown weak, boy. Used to be, you put your life on the line each time you took up the bow. Not anymore."

At some point in the story, Jabi said something like this to Bisco. Something felt strange about it when I wrote it, but I ignored the feeling and pressed on.

"You've forgotten to pray for yourself. You've forgotten that you're nothing but an arrow."

After I wrote these words, I realized what I was feeling. It was as if the old man was speaking through Bisco, directly to me. He was warning me, through the monitor that displayed my own story. I can't imagine that's an experience that most people share.

I must admit that Bisco contains traces of my own spiritual outlook. In the first volume, he gains a trusted partner and fulfills his role as an "arrow." In the second and third volumes, he spreads his prayers, makes new friends, and finds validation in the world. In the fourth and fifth volumes, he becomes akin to a god, protecting people for their sakes, and not just for his own.

It was a natural progression, I thought, but here Jabi warned me. "You are not a god—you are an arrow." As if telling me not to grow too big for my boots, not to take the easy path...

But I wasn't sure what to do about that.

And so I decided to see what Bisco had to say.

Bisco, in turn, decided to merge the good points of both "arrow" and "god." He decided to be both hungry and full at the same time. It was a new kind of middle ground, outside the normal bounds of morality, that Bisco alone came up with.

Well, that's not good. You're not even an adult yet.

In any case, to turn this philosophy into a weapon, Bisco was granted the *Ultrafaith Arrow*. This ability has the power to rewrite the rules of reality according to its bearer's desires. (Yeah, it's a bit overpowered.)

But in truth, anyone with a kind and strong will, with a philosophy like Bisco's, can do anything. Even if it takes a very long time.

So yeah. I guess it's fine. (Sorry, that's a bit of a cop-out…)

Bisco is always a few steps ahead of me. Of course, Bisco is a reflection of the kind of person I'd like to be, so that makes perfect sense. But I can't let him get too far ahead of me, or I won't be able to write him anymore.

When I think back to the day I sent in my half-baked manuscript for a shot at the grand prize, I can't help marveling at how far I've come. Perhaps I'll catch up with him yet.

In any case, see you next time.

—Shinji Cobkubo

SHINJI COBKUBO PRESENTS

NEXT TIME

The boys' adventures continue in...

The Rust Wind eats away at the world. A boy with a bow matches its ferocity.